DEATH IN PICCADILLY

A 1930s Mystery

Peter Zander-Howell

Copyright © 2025 Peter Zander-Howell

All rights reserved

Certain well-known historical persons are mentioned in this work. All other characters and events portrayed in this book are fictitious, and any similarity to real persons, alive or dead, is coincidental and not intended by the author. Real-world locations in this book may have been slightly altered.

No part of this book may be reproduced, or stored in a retrieval system, or transmitted in any form or by any means, electronic, mechanical, photocopying, recording, or otherwise, without the express permission of the publisher.

Cover image © The Francis Frith Collection

ISBN - 9798317440220

CONTENTS

Title Page
Copyright
CHAPTER 1   1
CHAPTER 2   8
CHAPTER 3   14
CHAPTER 4   19
CHAPTER 5   23
CHAPTER 6   38
CHAPTER 7   53
CHAPTER 8   64
CHAPTER 9   70
CHAPTER 10   80
CHAPTER 11   90
CHAPTER 12   98
CHAPTER 13   112
CHAPTER 14   124
CHAPTER 15   133

CHAPTER 16	144
CHAPTER 17	154
Books By This Author	167

CHAPTER 1

Wednesday August 30th, 1939

In a huge house on London's Hyde Park Corner, maids were busy taking early morning tea into the bedrooms of the owner and her guests.

At a quarter past seven, eighteen-year-old Niamh O'Brien tapped on the Honourable Jocelyn Hardingham's door and walked in. In the gloomy light she placed the tray on the bedside table, and moved across the room to draw the curtains. She spent half a minute at the window, notionally tidying the drapes but actually watching the traffic at the junction. At this time of day, most vehicles – cars, buses, vans and a few horse-drawn wagons were travelling from her right to left, from Knightsbridge towards the centre of the city. About half of them continued into Piccadilly, with some turning down Grosvenor Place towards Victoria, and a handful going down Constitution Hill past Buckingham Palace.

A pity, she thought, that no trams passed this way; she loved the rattly vehicles, but the West End was almost devoid of what seemed to be regarded as a plebeian form of public transport.

Niamh thought how wonderful it would be to be able to sit at this first-floor window for an hour or so, and just watch the moving panorama. She would never have believed anyone who told her that twenty years later her mistress's imposing house and its neighbours would all be demolished, and that little Park Lane would burst through where they had stood, and become an important input to the junction. Indeed, the only one of this row of great properties to survive would be Apsley House at 149 Piccadilly – more commonly known as Number 1, London.

Having no further excuse for window-gazing, Niamh turned back into the room. The occupant hadn't stirred, and the maid now saw that he was lying face upward. She could see that his eyes were open, but they were not looking at her.

Hesitantly, she moved nearer the bed, and quickly realised that something was seriously wrong. She had never seen a dead person before, and hesitantly reached down and touched his forehead. It was cold.

Niamh ran out of the room, down two flights of stairs, and burst into the huge kitchen.

Only two people were present, most of the staff being engaged on various duties. The Butler, Mr Morgan, was sitting at the table just starting his own breakfast. Mrs Warren, the Cook, was busy at the big range.

Niamh blurted out her news.

"Oh dearie me!" exclaimed the Cook, "he can't be above thirty. Are you sure he's dead?"

Niamh, now in tears, insisted that she was sure.

Morgan grunted crossly but said nothing. However, he noticeably speeded up his eating process.

Sit down, Niamh, and I'll pour you a cup of tea," instructed Mrs Warren.

By the time this was done, Morgan had emptied his plate.

"I'll go and verify what you say," he announced, and putting on his jacket stalked out of the room.

Within a minute, other servants began to return to the kitchen, and soon three of the four housemaids and one of the three footmen were present. Niamh was too upset to speak, but Mrs Warren passed on the news to each newcomer – and a buzz of conversation ensued.

When the Butler returned, the sound died away, and everyone looked at him.

"Mr Hardingham has indeed passed on," he intoned. "Florence, go to your mistress's room and ask if she will see me for a minute. I'll wait outside."

Evelyn Forbes-Kerr's bedroom was on the same floor as Mr Hardingham's, but faced the rear, looking out over Hyde Park and East Carriage Drive. The patrician-looking woman, now in her seventieth year, was sitting up in bed, enjoying her cup of tea. On hearing Florence's unprecedented request, she immediately told the girl to send the Butler in.

Morgan entered the bedroom, but remained standing by the door. He explained the situation in two sentences.

"Extraordinary," remarked his mistress. "A stroke or heart failure, I suppose. Better call Doctor Knowles, Morgan."

"Very good, madam."

Morgan and Florence left the room and went down one floor. Here the Butler stopped by the hall telephone, while the maid went through to the back stairs and descended to the kitchen again.

Dr Andrew Knowles had a consulting room in his Down Street house, but saw only a handful of patients there each week. His practice consisted mainly of visiting the houses of the rich, and Mrs Forbes-Kerr was typical of those on his list.

He was having his own breakfast when his own servant called him to the telephone. After hearing what Morgan had to say, the doctor said he would call within half an hour.

"What's the weather like, James?" he asked the servant as he resumed his meal.

"Very pleasant, sir. Likely to be a warm and dry day," replied the man.

"Good. I'm going to Douglas House after breakfast; it's only a few hundred yards, so I'll walk."

After finishing his meal, Knowles picked up his medical bag from the hall table, took a hat from the stand, and left by the front door.

He arrived at the Forbes-Kerr residence, and was admitted by Samuel Owen, one of the footmen. He knew the doctor as a regular caller, and took his hat.

"My instructions are to escort you upstairs, sir, and when you have finished Madam asks you to join her and her guests at breakfast – at least for a cup of coffee if you don't wish to eat."

"Lead on then Samuel."

As the two started up the stairs, Knowles enquired about the presence of guests.

"It's out of season, Samuel; isn't your mistress usually in the country through August and September?"

"Not so much these days, sir. Her husband died ten years ago, as you will know, and since then she has favoured the town over the country more and more. Half of Morlands is more-or-less shut up now – she was down for a week at the beginning of this month, but that's her only visit this year. Mr Morgan said she told him recently she would like to sell it, but that there is no market for such places at present.

"Anyway," continued the footman as he opened Hardingham's door and stood aside, "she held a dinner party last night. Nine of her thirteen guests are staying overnight – including of course Mr Hardingham."

Knowles advanced to the bed, and peered at the occupant. He then put down his bag, and turned back to the footman, still standing by the door.

"Leave me, Samuel. I'll find my own way down when I've finished. Close the door behind you."

Left alone, Knowles pulled back the bedclothes, revealing – to his surprise – that not only was the body not wearing pyjamas, but it was partially arrayed in evening clothes – dress shirt with no tie, vest, underpants, and socks.

The Doctor glanced around the room. A pair of evening trousers, braces still attached, hung neatly over the back of a chair. A black tie lay on the dressing table. Through the open door of a wardrobe Knowles thought he could see the associated dinner jacket on a coat hanger.

Frowning, he turned back to the body, and with some difficulty rolled it over in order to take the rectal temperature. He immediately saw to his astonishment how the man had died, and paused to think. He looked around the room again, this time looking down at the carpet. Within seconds he stopped, and turned his attention back to the dead man.

He took the temperature, and after making some notes in a pocketbook, he repacked his bag. He considered whether to draw a sheet over the body, but decided against, and moved to the door. He removed the key from the inside, and left the bedroom, locking the door from the outside and slipping the key in his pocket.

The Doctor was sufficiently familiar with the house to know that there was a telephone in the study in addition to the one in the hall. Going quickly down the main staircase, he went into the study, and closed the door behind him.

Sitting down at the desk, he picked up the handset, and when the operator responded, asked her to connect him with Vine Street police station. The switchboard woman there put him through to CID as he requested, and he then spoke to a detective sergeant. The Doctor quickly identified himself, and took only two minutes to explain what he had found. The sergeant said he would pass the matter on to his superior immediately. Knowles said he would remain on site until the police arrived.

CHAPTER 2

Putting down the telephone, Knowles left the study. He had never been invited even to dine in the great house, let alone to stay overnight, and so didn't know which were the breakfast and dining rooms. There was no sign of anyone – guest or servant – in the hall, but he could hear muffled voices coming through a door almost opposite the study. He opened the door and looked inside. At a table, large but not as large as he had expected, sat six people. A maid and a footman stood by a sideboard, on which he could see the usual breakfast dishes, the hot ones under silver covers.

"Ah, Doctor, good morning," called the hostess, seated at the head of the breakfast table. "Come and take a seat. Would you care to eat?"

"Just a strong coffee, please, Mrs Forbes-Kerr; I have already had breakfast."

"Of course. Estelle, coffee for the Doctor, please."

Knowles sat down between a woman in her late eighties and a young lady who looked to be little over twenty.

"Let me introduce you," said the hostess. "Everyone, this is Doctor Knowles – he takes care of my various ailments. Doctor, to your right is Mrs Fitzwallace, next to her is Mr Crampton, then Lady Wymondham, Mr Blanchflower, me you know, and to your left is Miss Wren. Apart from Jocelyn Hardingham, I have two other guests who will probably come down in the next few minutes."

In lieu of rising and moving around the table to shake hands, Crampton and Blanchflower each lifted a hand in acknowledgement.

The footman deftly removed the plate in front of Knowles, as the maid put a cup of coffee down in its place.

"Now, the business of Jocelyn is very sad, of course," continued the hostess. "What was wrong with him? I'll have to call his parents shortly and break the news."

The Doctor hesitated. "I had hoped to be able to tell you about it privately," he temporised.

"Oh rubbish, man – we're all friends here. And you can speak in front of the servants even if you're going to say that he died from congenital syphilis or something equally embarrassing."

"Nothing like that. Worse, really. He was shot dead. Evidently not self-inflicted."

There was a shocked silence for a moment. Then Blanchflower, a hard-faced bald-headed man of fifty, spoke.

"I'm not for a moment suggesting that Hardingham did commit suicide," he said, "but how do you know he didn't?"

"Several reasons. No weapon in the room, for a start – and he was shot in the back of his head, an impossibility for someone committing suicide."

There was another silence. This time Knowles was the one to break it.

"There's something else which negates any chance of suicide, ladies and gentlemen. Mr Hardingham was clearly in the process of getting ready for bed, but had only half undressed. He had taken off his jacket, tie, and trousers, but he was still wearing shirt and undergarments. After he was killed, someone lifted his body onto the bed, and pulled up the bedclothes.

"I have of course notified the police."

There was yet another silence, as those around the table digested what Knowles had said. Before anyone spoke again, the door opened and two more men entered the room.

"'Morning Evelyn," said the first man cheerily, and this was repeated by the second almost in unison.

Immediately after issuing their greeting, both newcomers realised that there was a silence, and that every face was long. They also saw the stranger at the table.

The hostess pulled herself together.

"Sorry Andrew, Travis – this is Doctor Knowles," she said. "Doctor – Lord Wymondham and Mr Egerton."

This time, as both men were close to the Doctor, he rose and shook hands. Wymondham was a tall, pleasant-faced man with curly black hair. In his early sixties, he looked to be a few years older than his wife. Egerton was much the same age, bald as the proverbial coot, but making up for that by sporting a somewhat incongruous blonde moustache.

"Sort out your breakfasts, and then you must hear what we've just been told," directed Mrs Forbes-Kerr.

Wymondham asked for tea, and Egerton coffee. Both declined the offer of porridge, and went straight to the sideboard where each helped himself to a plate of hot food. Egerton's selection was especially biased towards kidneys and bacon, while Wymondham clearly enjoyed sausages, scrambled eggs, and fried bread.

They took their seats again and began to eat, both looking towards their hostess as they did so.

Before she could speak again, Egerton suddenly let out a whistle.

"I say," he exclaimed, "the Doctor chappie is sitting where Hardingham should be. The poor man's ill, I take it?"

"Explain, Doctor, please," instructed Mrs Forbes-Kerr.

Knowles went quickly through the basics again.

"Good God," muttered Egerton, and something very similar was heard from Lord

Wymondham.

The girl next to Knowles spoke for the first time.

"What sort of gun was used, Doctor? Not a shotgun, surely? But whatever it was, some of us should have heard the shot – I mean, my room is next to his, and I didn't hear a thing."

"The walls in this house are very thick, Phoebe, as are the doors," commented the hostess.

"I understand that, Evelyn, but the weather is warm – I had windows open in my bedroom, and I guess Jocelyn would too."

"The weapon used was a small-calibre pistol, Miss Wren," said Knowles. "I believe there are models which can be fitted with a silencer. I rather think that the shot would have made very little noise – certainly it wouldn't have sounded like a gun firing. And Hyde Park Corner is an exceptionally busy junction, so presumably there is always traffic noise outside.

"Also, perhaps even more pertinent, it may be that this happened before you went to bed."

There was another silence.

"Well," said the elderly Mrs Fitzwallace, also speaking for the first time, "to borrow a word – or phrase – from detective novels, whodunnit? Must be one of your valued guests, Evelyn," she added maliciously, a wicked grin only slightly tempering the words. "Not necessarily one who stayed overnight, though – it could have been someone just here for dinner. I noticed that Jocelyn retired very early, before anyone had left."

These remarks caused another silence around the table, each person lost in his or her own thoughts.

Knowles, who knew nothing about Hardingham or indeed any of the other guests, hadn't been wasting his time looking around the table to see if he could see any sign of guilt, and now he learned that there were even more suspects there was even less point in doing so.

He signalled wordlessly to Estelle that he would like more coffee. The maid, who like the footman was still shocked by what she had heard, hurried around the table with the coffee pot.

CHAPTER 3

Within minutes of the call to Vine Street, the report was moving up through the police ranks rapidly. The sergeant to whom Knowles had spoken was familiar with the Piccadilly address, and knew that the occupant was one of the great hostesses in the area around Mayfair. He was aware that the sort of visitors regularly seen at this house included cabinet ministers, peers of the realm, very wealthy men, and even royalty. He decided to advise his Superintendent at once.

The Super, equally familiar with the name of the householder, made the instant decision that C Division wasn't the right outfit to handle this case. As soon as he ended the call to the DS he called Chief Superintendent Mayhew at New Scotland Yard.

Mayhew didn't know the particular house, although he was aware that some of the great socialite hostesses like Lady Cunard and Mrs Laura Corrigan lived in the area, but he had certainly heard the name Evelyn Forbes-Kerr. He agreed to take on the case, and made three quick calls.

The first was to summon Detective Chief

Inspector David Adair. Adair had been hoping for a quiet day in the office clearing some paperwork, and sighed audibly as he put down the telephone, and stood up to make the journey to his boss's office.

The second call was to St George's Hospital, where he asked to speak to a senior forensic pathologist – a man the Yard had employed before. He was lucky to be connected within seconds, and the Doctor agreed to help. He laughed on being told the location of the body, and said as the hospital was less than a hundred yards away he'd be there within half an hour, after finishing some other work.

The third call was to brief the Assistant Commissioner (Crime). The AC, always alert to potential problems such as those likely to arise when influential people crossed the path of the police, concurred with Mayhew's decisions, and asked to be kept informed.

In fact, after putting down the telephone, he thought for a few seconds, and then he too stood up and made his way down to the Chief Superintendent's office.

It was only twenty minutes after Knowles' call that Adair and the AC arrived at the Chief Super's room together.

"Put Adair in the picture, Mayhew," instructed the senior officer when all three had sat down.

"Body of a man found at Douglas House,

Piccadilly. A guest. Shot in the back of the head in his bedroom, then apparently put into bed. Cause of death wasn't apparent initially, so a local doctor was called. He discovered what had happened and called Vine Street, but C Division thinks the Yard should take this one on. This is going to be your job."

He paused.

Adair, realising that the AC wasn't present by coincidence, and having vaguely heard of Douglas House, guessed that the matter was one which would require delicate handling because influential people were involved. This was quickly confirmed.

Mrs Forbes-Kerr is one of London's top society hostesses," said the AC. She lives almost next door to Apsley House – the Duke of Wellington's town house, you know – and her dinners and parties are legendary. She knows everyone who counts. This investigation will need tact, Adair – but it must still be done thoroughly and without fear or favour."

Mayhew resumed.

"Doctor Knowles reported that a footman told him there was a dinner party in the house last night, and that nine of the thirteen guests had stayed overnight.

"The dead man is the Honourable Jocelyn Hardingham, son of Viscount Hardingham. The father, although in the Lords, is a Minister of State at the Foreign Office. That's all we know.

"Who will you take with you?"

The DCI hesitated. "DI Davison is away on holiday, and won't be back for several days. I have two sergeants, Gemmill and Borthwick. They're both competent. But this is a job where it'd be handy to have someone who moves in these sort of circles, gentlemen. Can I have that new DI who's just come through the Trenchard scheme, young Bryce? I know he's a Cambridge-educated barrister, and I believe he comes from a landed background – he'd be very useful. Must be a good copper too," he added, "the award of the King's Police Medal is a rare occurrence."

"You could have had him if he was available," replied Mayhew, "but he isn't. He's down to give evidence today and probably tomorrow at the Old Bailey – and as he's also the case officer he's likely to be tied up there for a week.

"You'll have to make do with your sergeants. But anyway, Adair, you don't exactly come from an impoverished background yourself – and the praise that was heaped on you from that earl and from the wealthy middle-eastern gentlemen after that kidnapping case shows that you can get on perfectly well with the rich and mighty!

"Off you go, and keep me informed."

"Yes," added the AC, "and although I don't anticipate any interference from powerful people, report immediately if there is any."

The DCI returned to his office. As he passed his Secretary's desk he asked her to call Messrs

Borthwick and Gemmill and tell them to come up at once.

The two sergeants were of similar build, both being squat and sturdy, and of the same age – 30.

It took Adair only a minute to pass on the very limited information he had, and the three men were soon on their way to Douglas House.

CHAPTER 4

DS Gemmill, who was driving an unmarked Railton Cobham police car on loan from the Flying Squad, parked with some difficulty in front of Douglas House. The three detectives walked up the steps to the imposing front door, and Adair pulled the bell handle.

After a minute, the door swung open, and a man who could only have been the Butler greeted them.

"Good morning, gentlemen; you are no doubt the Scotland Yard officers. Please come in."

In the large hallway, the DCI identified himself and his colleagues.

"Both medical gentlemen are viewing the body, sir. I'll show you up, if you will follow me."

As they all ascended the staircase, Morgan continued, speaking over his shoulder.

"When you have finished in the bedroom, my instructions are to show your subordinates to the study – which the mistress has designated for your use – and I am then to take you to meet her in the morning room, after which she will introduce you to other guests in the drawing room.

"This is Mr Hardingham's room, sirs. When you are ready to go down, just ring the bell and I or a footman will return."

He tapped on the door, and opened it without waiting for a reply. He then stood aside for the policemen to enter.

The three went into the room, and the Butler closed the door behind them.

"'Morning David," said the pathologist, standing up from where he had been leaning over the body on the bed. "A few months since I've seen you! This is Doctor Knowles – he was called before anyone realised this was a murder. Knowles, this is DCI Adair, and if I remember correctly sergeants Borthwick and Gemmill."

"Good memory, Tim," said Adair, shaking hands with Doctor Knowles. "What do you want to tell us?"

"Well, the two of us aren't going to argue about cause or time of death. The man was shot in the head from behind. Between half past nine last night and one o'clock this morning. When I get him on the slab I might narrow that down a bit, perhaps to between ten-thirty and eleven thirty.

"It was a small calibre weapon, probably a point two-two pistol, and presumably fitted with a suppressor, as nobody seems to have heard a shot. The bullet is still inside the head. We've looked around, under the bed and so on, but there's no sign of a gun.

"I haven't looked in his suitcase, but there is a set of keys on the bedside table.

"The only other thing – and again the two of us are agreed – is that he was shot while over there by the dressing table. There wasn't much bleeding, but there are some drops on the floor by that stool.

"For some reason the man was then placed face up on the bed, still wearing half of his evening clothes."

"That's right," said Knowles, "and the bedclothes were then pulled up to his chin."

Adair eyed the tea tray still placed beside the keys on the bedside table, as he pressed the electric bell push beside the bed.

"This is hearsay, Chief Inspector," said Knowles, "but the footman who showed me up said that the maid who brought the tea didn't immediately realise Hardingham was dead. When she did, she ran down to raise the alarm, and the Butler came up to check. Neither realised the man had been shot – and neither did I until I turned the body over to take a rectal reading.

"When I saw the bullet hole, I locked the door and gave instructions that nobody was to attempt to get in here – so of course the tray is untouched."

"Quite right to keep everyone out, Doctor. All right.

"Tim, will you make arrangements to get the body removed? Gemmill, please take Doctor Knowles to the study, and take a statement.

Borthwick, you stay in here and look around. Search the suitcase of course. Take some photographs, and make notes of everything relevant. Find your way to the study when you've finished, or ring for a guide again. I'll take the keys now."

A tap at the door signified the return of Morgan. All except Borthwick followed him down the stairs.

"Is there a telephone in the study?" enquired Adair.

"Yes, sir, there is."

"Right, if you don't mind us using it first, Tim, I want to call for reinforcements. Gemmill, get on to the office and find any two DCs – or anyone – who can come at once and help search the house. Then when you've taken Dr Knowles statement, work out a plan for going over the house. Perhaps Mr Morgan here can supply you with a maid or someone as guide."

"That will be no problem, sir," replied the Butler, as he showed the two doctors and one policeman to the study. He then took Adair further along a corridor and tapped on another door. Again opening it without waiting for a response to the knock, he led the way inside.

"Detective Chief Inspector Adair, madam," he said, bowing very slightly.

CHAPTER 5

Mrs Forbes-Kerr was sitting at a writing table. Nobody else was in the room.

"Ah, do come and sit down, Chief Inspector. Are both doctors still here, Morgan?"

Yes, madam. The Pathologist is making a telephone call to arrange about the body, and Doctor Knowles is making a statement."

Good – I don't need to see Knowles again, so just tell him to send his bill as usual. If the Chief Inspector has finished with them, just let both doctors out when they are ready. That will be all, Morgan."

While the householder had been speaking, Adair was appraising her. He saw a very elegant lady – patrician was the obvious word which came to mind – of about seventy, dressed in white blouse and long black skirt. No jewellery was visible at all, save for a wedding ring on her left hand. Her hair was completely white, and she had a lorgnette hanging from a cord around her neck. She had not risen when Adair came in, but he could see she was tall – he guessed she would top his own five foot seven.

With Morgan gone, she turned to the DCI.

"A very nasty business, Mr Adair. Let me say at the outset that I have no idea who might have killed poor Jocelyn. Frankly, although I have to accept that one of my guests must be a murderer, I am finding that concept difficult to comprehend.

"I only know the little that Dr Knowles was able to tell us at breakfast. I gather that Jocelyn was shot, and that the body was then moved?"

"That is so, ma'am. As yet we have no idea why it was put into bed – it confused your maid when she brought the tea, and also your butler, when he went to check. But it could only have delayed discovery by a matter of minutes."

"Indeed. What about the weapon?"

"A small-calibre pistol, almost certainly fitted with a silencer. Do you have firearms in the house, ma'am?"

"None at all. My late husband had various firearms. I remember in particular his revolver, left over from when he was in the army in the 1880s and 1890s, because he sometimes used to shoot with it at a target on the lawn. And he owned several shotguns. But they're all at Morlands, my country house – we've never kept guns here. Your uniformed colleagues might look askance if we did a bit of duck shooting in Hyde Park!

"I was never very interested in guns, although fifty years ago when I was first married I used to take a four-ten out to go after rabbits and pigeons occasionally. Since Frederick died ten years ago, I haven't even set foot in the gun room at Morlands. And probably not for five or six years before that. I suppose his collection is still intact. However, I never heard him mention anything with a silencer."

"What can you tell me about the victim, ma'am?"

"A very personable young man. Thirty now, I think, and still unmarried. Actually, I haven't really seen him since he was at school. He read Greats at Oxford, and at that time his name was linked to various debs. But I suppose he prefers to play the field, as the saying goes. After university I think he went to help at a small publishing house for a bit. The family has money, of course, so he hasn't really had to work. His father – Lord Hardingham – is at the Foreign Office. He sent Jocelyn abroad for a year or so. He's only been back in England for a few weeks.

"To be honest, I thought of him a couple of months ago, when an old friend of mine said she hoped her granddaughter – young Phoebe Wren – might find a nice young man a few years older than herself. So I invited him and her to dinner last night, even though they are far younger than the guests I usually entertain. I hoped he might take an interest in Phoebe. They hadn't met before – she only came out this year, and apparently he was abroad then. And he did take an interest in her. Alas, Phoebe didn't seem to like him at all. A pity –

it would have been an eminently suitable match."

"Have Mr Hardingham's parents been informed of his death – and of the circumstances?"

"Yes. I telephoned Edwin Hardingham as soon as I knew his son was dead. He was upset, of course. Merle was at home, and Edwin undertook to break the news to her at once."

"I understand that some but not all of your dinner guests stayed overnight?"

"That is so. Fourteen of us sat down to dinner, and ten slept here. Or, if Jocelyn died before actually going to bed, I suppose I should say nine slept here.

"Now, you'll want to know who was in the house at the time this ghastly crime was committed – but I don't know what time that was. It could be that some of my guests were safely away before Jocelyn was shot."

"The doctors have given a provisional time of death – or rather a range of times. It was between half past nine and one o'clock. The Pathologist expects to narrow that down – perhaps to between half past ten and half past eleven."

Mrs Forbes-Kerr was silent for a minute.

"I see," she said at last. "Well, none of the guests who weren't staying overnight left the house before half past eleven. In fact all four left at the same time, at about twenty to midnight. Morgan may be able to give you an accurate time. However, it looks as though none of my guests can put forward the alibi of absence.

"Anyway, anticipating that you will need to know who was in the house, I have drawn up a comprehensive list."

She pushed a paper across the table to the DCI.

"Perhaps it would help if I go through the list and give you a brief indication of who these people are."

Adair nodded, and looked down at the list, neatly handwritten in violet ink.

Guests:
The Honourable Jocelyn Hardingham (deceased)
Mr & Mrs Mark Routledge
Sir Oliver and Lady Easton
Mr Patrick Crampton
Mrs Ada Fitzwallace
The Marquis & Marchioness of Wymondham
Miss Phoebe Wren
Mr Travis Egerton
Mrs Esmeralda Wilcox
Mr Ralph Blanchflower
Employees:
Miss Eileen Barnes (secretary)
Mr Richard Morgan (butler)
Mrs Dorcas Warren (cook)
Samuel Owen (footman)
Matthew Walsh (footman)
Patrick Rafferty (footman)
Niamh O'Brien (maid)
Florence Stone (maid)

Estelle Bates (maid)
Bernice Long (maid)
John Higgins (boot boy and general factotum)

"There's me as well, of course," said the hostess. I'm the relict of the late Frederick Forbes-Kerr, a politician of whom you may have heard. He was a Government minister, and died in office. A tragedy for me, of course, and perhaps for the country – he might well have become prime minister.

Then Jocelyn. He was Edwin Hardingham's elder son, and heir to the viscountcy. The heir is now the younger son, Inigo, who has just finished his second year at Cambridge. He's quite a different character – a very shy young man, I'm told. Edwin is my guest occasionally, but Jocelyn has never been here before.

Next comes Sir Oliver Easton and his wife Adele. Oliver is my brother – he's the eleventh baronet. I'm older than him, so if I'd been born a boy the baronetcy would be mine. They never stay the night when they visit, as they live only a few hundred yards away.

"Mr & Mrs Routledge. Mark is a banker, and also holds directorships in half a dozen companies. I was at school with Patricia well over fifty years ago, and we've been friends ever since. Come to that, I've known Mark nearly as long – he was a deb's delight when she and I came out in May 1889."

The DCI smiled inwardly at hearing this term. He had assumed it was a somewhat derogatory one used by the newspapers, and hadn't realised that participants employed the term themselves.

"Patrick Crampton is an up-and-coming barrister. He's in his early forties, and took silk about five years ago. It is expected that he'll be appointed as a High Court judge quite soon. He served with great distinction in the war, winning the DSO and MC. He is married, but Deidre wasn't able to join us yesterday – she is away in Cornwall visiting her mother. Patrick stayed the night."

Adair cynically thought that Crampton's chance of elevation to the Bench might well be improved by moving in Mrs Forbes-Kerr's social circle, but he said nothing.

"Ada Fitzwallace is actually my sister-in-law – my late husband was a few years older than I, and Ada is his elder sister. Her own husband died seven or eight years ago. She lives in Royal Tunbridge Wells, and will stay here for a few more days.

"Then we have Andrew and Elizabeth Fox-Gilbert, Marquis and Marchioness of Wymondham. Although the marquisate is attached to the small Norfolk town, they actually live in Hampshire, and both stayed here last night. Despite the fact that my husband was some ten years older than Andrew, they worked together for a number of years and became close friends.

"I've mentioned Phoebe. She's the only

daughter of the Earl of Ablington, so she's actually Lady Phoebe Wren – but she refuses to use her courtesy title – insists on 'miss'. She is at university in Durham.

"Travis Egerton is a fascinating man. He can talk to anyone on any subject. He's an international businessman, with fingers in many pies. He has interests in oil, in rubber, and in shipping – just to give a few examples. I'm a rich woman, but I guess he could buy me out from his small change. He is on familiar terms with the most disparate lot of people – the American President, the Duke of Windsor, King Ibn Saud, and so on. But I've heard a taxi driver address him as 'Mr Egerton', and Travis replied using the man's Christian name, and they had a very friendly chat about the requirements for doing the 'knowledge'! A true gentleman in every sense of the word.

"He doesn't have a house in London, but keeps a permanent suite at Claridges. However, he stayed here last night and will be here for a few more days, on holiday really, before flying from Croydon to Paris on Monday.

"Esmeralda Wilcox is an MP, as you probably know. We won't have a female prime minister in my lifetime, but she would be a good candidate. She is an old school friend of my daughter, so I've known her for years. Her constituency is two hundred miles away in the north of England, and when Parliament is in session she has been staying alternately with Patricia and me until she can sort out a suitable flat in town.

"Finally, Ralph Blanchflower. You've probably heard of him too. He's the author of several books. But he's also a leader writer for the Daily Telegraph, and as such is a very influential man. He has a set in Albany, within walking distance, and hadn't intended to stay here overnight. But he didn't feel well after dinner and I suggested he should let us find him a bed."

Mrs Forbes-Kerr stopped, and watched the DCI finish scribbling on his pad.

"Very useful, ma'am. I see you've listed your servants too – is there anything particular I should know about any of them?"

"I don't think so. Morgan was a footman here before the war. After serving in the army, he came back and almost immediately was promoted to Butler when his predecessor retired in 1919. The others have served for varying periods, but nobody has been with me for less than a year. Bernice is the most recent appointment. Oh no, I forgot Higgins the boot boy – he came four or five months ago.

"I've included Eileen Barnes, my Secretary, in the list of employees although she is what is usually termed a 'distressed gentlewoman' and isn't a servant in the normal sense. She does sometimes join in a dinner party, but her presence yesterday would have meant an odd number at the table, so she would have been served a meal in her room – she doesn't eat with the servants, of course.

"I also have two scullery maids. They don't live in. One comes in six times a week, and the other when I've held a function of some sort. Both were present during the afternoon, but they would have left before we sat down to dinner. Morgan will confirm the times."

"Do any of your guests bring their own valets, or ladies' maids?"

"That is the case occasionally, but not this time. All my regular guests know that I can provide a footman – usually Matthew – to act as valet, and a maid – usually Florence – to assist a female guest if required.

"It pains me deeply to say this, Chief Inspector, but one of my friends has to be responsible for this – there is no way that any of my servants could have even known Jocelyn, let alone having a motive for killing him."

Adair nodded slowly.

"I've taken a lot of your time, ma'am. Just a few more questions, if I may.

"This was obviously a formal dinner – how long ago was it arranged?"

"I gave Eileen a provisional list of names six or seven weeks ago. She then starts to find out when people can attend. It was probably finalised a month ago.

"Actually, it was what my late husband would have called 'informal' – he died before black tie dinners really started to become acceptable in this country – 'a wretched American habit', he called them. But I rarely have 'white tie' functions now, unless a member of the Royal family or a rather particular ambassador is coming. Even the Duke of Wellington two houses along, and Lord Rothschild next door, no longer expect such formality when they dine here."

Once again the DCI smiled inwardly.

"What, if I may enquire, were the topics of discussion around the table and afterwards? Were there any disagreements, for example?"

Mrs Forbes-Kerr snorted. "I should expect robust discussions in my house, Chief Inspector, without ever having to worry that they would turn into fisticuffs – or murder. In fact, last night I don't recall much argument over anything. Over dinner the principal topic was, naturally, the prospect of war in Europe, and what the position of our government might or should be. And what attitude the Americans might take."

"So what time did you leave the dinner table, ma'am?

"I suppose it was at about a quarter past ten. The ladies left the men to their port and we came into the drawing room. But they didn't linger long – probably it was only fifteen minutes later that they all joined us again. I say 'all', but in fact most of them presumably visited the lavatory, as they trickled in one at a time. When Jocelyn came in he immediately said to me that he wanted to retire early – he apologised for leaving the gathering, but said he was very tired. He insisted that he didn't need anything.

"The rest of us were in groups of three or four – quite fluid, as some people – not all – moved around a bit. We went on until about a quarter to midnight, as I said before, when my brother said he wanted to get off home. That was the signal for the others to leave too, and it was also when Ralph Blanchflower told me he was feeling under the weather. Between you and me Chief Inspector, I think the problem was a surfeit of alcohol.

"So as soon as the Eastons and the Routledges had left, I got Morgan to arrange for a room for Ralph. That was quite difficult, actually, because we were already accommodating guests in the second-floor bedrooms.

"Ralph went upstairs shortly afterwards. The remaining eight of us carried on talking until about half past twelve, when we all retired.

"This morning, Morgan came to report Jocelyn's death while I was still in bed – at that time he had no idea it was murder, of course, so I told him to fetch Doctor Knowles."

"Are your guests – the ones who stayed overnight – still in the house?"

"Oh yes. They all appreciate that you'll want to interrogate them, and at present they're all in the drawing room. Not Eileen, actually – she is working in her little office. But Mr Blanchflower and Mrs Wilcox would like to get away as soon as possible, so if you could start with one of them?"

"Of course, ma'am. I don't expect to need to

talk to anyone for more than ten minutes, or so – and I'd prefer the word 'interview' to 'interrogate'!

"Thank you for providing your study for me to use. If I ring the bell, presumably a member of your staff will then find each guest as I want them?"

The hostess nodded. "Certainly. The study was my husband's retreat – I don't use it much myself. And you'll want tea or coffee and so on. If you ring, someone will bring you refreshments – and sandwiches and so on at lunchtime."

"Very kind, ma'am. Two final things. The body will be removed very shortly, and conveyed to St George's for the required *post mortem* examination. The Piccadilly Room must remain locked for the next day or so, in case we need to check it again.

"We have to try to find the pistol, so my men will be conducting a search of the premises – including, I'm afraid, your guests' rooms and luggage."

"I wish you luck with that, Chief Inspector. This is a very large house, and in each room there are numerous items behind or in which a small gun might be concealed. But I understand you have to look."

"Yes, and I think I should explain that to your guests at once. I wonder if I could just have a quick word with them as a group? No need to introduce them to me at this stage, that can wait until I see them individually."

"Yes, of course. Let's go along now."

Mrs Forbes-Kerr stood, proving that she was indeed taller than the DCI. She led the way out of the room and along the hallway.

In the huge drawing room, the four men and four women were spread around. One man was in an armchair reading The Times. Another was sitting by the garden windows, smoking a pipe. An elderly lady – the DCI deduced that this was Mrs Fitzwallace – appeared to be doing some crochet work. A very young woman was seated at a small writing table, pen in hand, and Adair assumed this was Miss Wren. The remaining four were together, apparently talking.

All looked with interest at the unprepossessing little man as he was escorted into the room. The four men rose to be introduced but the hostess waved them to sit down again.

"This is Detective Chief Inspector Adair, from Scotland Yard," she said. "He'll meet you all properly later, but just wants to say a few preliminary words now."

She remained standing, and Adair moved forward slightly.

"Good morning, ladies and gentlemen. This is a nasty business. I just want to say two things. Your hostess has passed on the request for two of you to be interviewed first, and that is fine. However, if anyone indicates now that they have some idea of who did this, please say, and he or she can jump the queue."

Nobody spoke, and two or three shook their heads.

"One other thing. In the next few minutes my men will start to search for the pistol used to kill Mr Hardingham. The search will include your bedrooms and your luggage."

"Inevitable, of course," muttered the pipe smoker, "and I guess it's no more intrusive than when one goes through customs checks in some European countries."

"Very true, Blanchflower," replied the Times reader. "Probably a lot less intrusive in fact. At least the English police won't act like many a foreign official – confiscating things like packets of cigarettes allegedly for being prohibited, but actually for their own personal benefit."

Adair smiled. "I guarantee that my men will be wholly professional. Anyway, thank you ladies and gentlemen. Let me get settled in the study, and I'll ask someone to fetch Mrs Wilcox in a few minutes."

CHAPTER 6

Adair made his way back to the study, where he found that both doctors had gone. Gemmill was poring over what was evidently a plan of the house, unfolded on the big desk. Standing beside him was a big-boned woman in her forties, dressed in a typical maid's costume.

"Hello, sir," the Sergeant greeted him. "Mr Morgan has found a plan to help us with the search, and this is Bernice, who is going to be our guide. Heck of a job, though – there are five storeys and the house is much deeper than I'd expected. Anyway, sir, Stone and Underwood will be here any minute."

"I agree it's not going to be an easy job – Mrs Forbes-Kerr said that to me only a minute ago. Anyway, we have to try.

"I'm grateful for your help, Bernice. We'll be talking to all the staff eventually, but what can you tell us about the late Mr Hardingham?"

"Nothing, sir, really. I'm a chambermaid. I help in the kitchen a bit, but I don't serve at table, so I haven't seen him this visit. In fact they tell me he's never stayed here before. They say he's a one for the ladies, sir, but I wouldn't know about that."

A jangle of the front door bell coincided with the entry of Sergeant Borthwick, who came into the room carrying what looked like a bath towel. He was just starting to speak when he realised the maid was present, and stopped in mid-sentence.

"Carry on, Sergeant," ordered the DCI. "Bernice, whatever you may hear must go no further, understand?"

The maid nodded, and Borthwick continued.

"This towel was neatly folded over the back of a chair by the dressing table, sir. As I moved the chair to look in the drawer, the towel fell off. I picked it up, and was just starting to fold it again to leave it as I found it, when I noticed this."

He quickly unfolded the towel, and showed his colleagues a hole in the material – with scorch marks around it.

"I guess this was the silencer, sir!"

Adair and Gemmill stared at the towel.

"I reckon you're right," replied Adair. "Well done."

He was about to add something when there was a tap on the door, and a uniformed footman appeared, leading two more men.

"Your extra policemen, sir," announced the footman.

"Thank you; that will be all."

"Welcome, Underwood and Stone. You're

here to search the house, looking for a small pistol. Sergeant Gemmill will explain where you need to go, and Bernice here will assist with who occupies each room. By the way, Sergeant, don't neglect the dustbins.

"Now, Borthwick and I will be interviewing in this room, so you can't come and go here. The four of you had better base yourselves in Mr Hardingham's bedroom. Carry on."

When the others had gone, the DCI pressed the bell push, and turned to Borthwick.

"Two of the guests want to leave as soon as possible, so we'll see them first. You take notes, as usual."

The same footman who had brought in the two constables now answered the bell.

"You rang, sir?"

"Yes. What is your name?"

"Samuel Owen, sir."

"All right, Samuel; please ask Mrs Wilcox to spare us a few minutes of her time. She is expecting the call."

The man bowed almost imperceptibly, and left the room. A minute later, a well-dressed woman of indeterminate age entered. She was wearing a long black skirt, a white high-necked blouse, and a light blue jacket. Like her hostess, the only jewellery visible was a pair of rings on her wedding finger. Adair and Borthwick had both risen as she came in.

"Mrs Wilcox, I presume," the DCI greeted

her. "This is Sergeant Borthwick." He indicated a chair in front of the desk. "Please take a seat."

Adair took the chair behind the desk, and the Sergeant sat down to one side, pulling out his pocketbook and a pencil as he did so.

"A novel experience for me," remarked the MP. "I think the only policemen I've ever spoken to before are the ones on duty in the Palace of Westminster – and they certainly don't question me!"

"I don't expect to ask many questions, ma'am. First, did you know Mr Hardingham well?"

"I didn't know him at all, Chief Inspector. I've met his father a couple of times – various parliamentary functions, you know – but not the son until yesterday."

"Talk me through what happened after dinner, please. The ladies left the gentlemen to their port, I understand. Then who did what?"

Mrs Wilcox described the movements, much as Mrs Forbes-Kerr had done earlier.

"Just a bit more detail, ma'am, if you will. Mr Hardingham came back into the drawing room after the meal. Who was still out of the room at that point?"

Mrs Wilcox considered the question.

"He came back at the same time as young Phoebe. I noticed particularly because he was smiling and she had a face like thunder. However, as I don't know either of them, and the lighting wasn't bright in the drawing room, perhaps I misinterpreted things.

"But he was the last of the men to return, and all the other females were already in the room."

"Thank you. Now, I understand that shortly after that, Mr Hardingham made his apologies, and went to bed early. Before he did that, did he sit down, or talk to anyone else in the room?"

"Definitely not. He went straight to Evelyn, said something about being tired, called 'goodnight everyone', and left the room. I suppose that was at about twenty to eleven."

"Good; thank you. Now, can you remember who left the room between then and the time when those who weren't staying overnight got up to leave?"

The MP thought about this for a few seconds before replying.

"I can tell you what I remember, but I can't say it's definitive. We weren't in a single group, you see. It's a big room, as you know, and we were sitting or standing in little groups – and moving about a bit too.

"During that period, Lord Wymondham left the room, and Phoebe went out again perhaps ten minutes after him. You're going to ask me how long they were away, but I can't say – I didn't notice when they returned.

"But anyway, as I say, one or more others could have gone out too.

"Evelyn's Doctor implied that Jocelyn was

killed quite soon after he went upstairs, in other words before any of the guests had left the house, and your questions seem to confirm that. All I can say is that I simply can't imagine either Andrew Wymondham or the Wren girl as a murderer."

"Well, ma'am, frankly at the moment I can't see why any of the guests should have killed Mr Hardingham. However, someone certainly did – and as your hostess said a few minutes ago, it has to be one of you."

Adair thought for a moment, and then came to a decision.

"All right, ma'am, that's all I need to ask. You are free to leave the house whenever you like. I imagine you'll be going back to the drawing room – please ask Mr Blanchflower to come and have a chat."

The detectives rose as Mrs Wilcox left the room.

"Any suspicious thoughts?" enquired Adair, as the door closed.

"No sir. Pure as the driven snow, I think. If it's true that she's never met him before, she can hardly have a motive."

The DCI grunted assent. The two men were still standing when their next interviewee arrived.

"I'm Ralph Blanchflower," announced the newcomer, offering his hand to the DCI. His bald head gleamed as the sun's rays streaming through the window caught it as he moved.

"Do sit down, sir," invited Adair, indicating

the chair recently vacated by Mrs Wilcox. "This won't take long, and then you are free to leave."

"Doubt if I can help much, Chief Inspector. Between you and me, I fear I had a few too many last night. Evelyn offered an excellent claret, some sort of dessert wine, vintage port, and brandy. So perhaps I won't remember things as clearly as I should."

Adair smiled politely.

"As best you can, then, if you please.

"First, how well did you know Mr Hardingham?"

"I'd only met him twice before, but at least five or six years ago. At some sort of party each time – don't remember where, but not in this house. We only spoke briefly, as I recall, and I certainly didn't know the man well.

"I knew of him, but that isn't quite the same."

"You mean you'd heard about him from others – was that before you actually met him, or more recently?"

"Both. But this is mere gossip, not evidence, Chief Inspector."

"No; but when searching for some sort of motive, one has to consider every snippet – and this is a case of murder. What was being said?"

"People say – and I repeat that I have no personal knowledge of this – that Hardingham was an immensely personable young man, but totally amoral. I can't say any more."

The DCI nodded slowly.

"Mrs Forbes-Kerr said he 'played the field' sir, so I suppose you are only backing up her statement. Anyway, I'm not sure that it helps us. Let's move on.

"Tell us about the movements of the various guests, including yourself, immediately after dinner."

Blanchflower's account concurred with that given by the others. Like Mrs Wilcox, he said that he couldn't guarantee that anyone other than Wymondham and Wren had left the drawing room in the period between Hardingham going to bed and the other guests leaving. However, he did add that each had been out of the room for about ten minutes.

"I'm not entirely stupid, Chief Inspector. You obviously believe that Hardingham was killed soon after he went to bed. Well, I certainly never left the drawing room in that period, and I'm sure others will be able to confirm that."

"I'm sure they will, sir. That's all I want to ask. Perhaps you will ask Miss Wren to join us if you see her."

As Blanchflower left the room, Sergeant Gemmill came in, followed by the two DCs. All looked happy, and as soon as the study door closed, Gemmill placed an object wrapped in cloth on the desk in front of his boss. He carefully pulled back the covering, revealing a very small automatic pistol, and a single brass cartridge case.

All five detectives gazed at these items silently for some seconds.

"Where was the pistol, and who found it?" enquired Adair.

"I did, sir," replied Gemmill. "We went to Hardingham's room as you suggested, to sort out who was going where. As all four of us came out, I noticed this huge sort of urn thing, on a table in the passageway not twenty feet from the deceased's bedroom. I thought it was worth a look, and took off the lid and reached inside. My fingers just touched metal, so we turned the thing over and the pistol slid out without needing to handle it. The cartridge came out too.

"As we came down the stairs we saw one of your interviewees arrive, and I thought we'd best wait until he came out rather than disturb you. I sent Bernice back to her duties."

"Well done indeed, Sergeant. Not much doubt that this is the murder weapon."

"But what is it, sir?" enquired Borthwick. "It would easily fit in the palm of my hand."

"It's a German Liliput – note two 'ells' not three – by August Menz. The Yard Armourer has one of these – but his is a rarer one with a nickel finish, whereas this is the more usual model in blued steel. He won't allow anyone to fire the one in his collection, alas.

"This one was made in 1927 – you can see the date stamp. From what Inspector Brough told me, they were only made between about 1920 and

1930.

"But if you think this is small – and 6.35 mm is certainly a small calibre – the Menz company made an even smaller model of only 4.25 mm."

Adair suddenly realised he and his colleagues had been so engrossed with the automatic that none of them had noticed Miss Wren entering the study. She was also looking at the pistol, and listening to him talking."

"Apologies, Miss Wren; I didn't see you come in. Please take a seat here at the desk; I'll not be a minute.

"Underwood, Stone, you can return to your other duties; sorry it's been a waste of your time. Gemmill, go back to the Yard with them. Take the pistol to Inspector Brough. The safety catch is on, but don't touch the thing yourself. Mr Brough once told me a story about a man who had one of these things in his pocket. It went off accidentally, and shot him in the opposite knee. Although come to think of it that might have been a Hungarian Liliput, which is a different beast. Anyway, make sure this thing isn't pointing at anyone until the Armourer unloads it. Ask him to see what he can find in the way of prints. I don't hold out much hope on the gun itself – you certainly couldn't leave prints on the knurled rubber butt. However, the magazine has a lovely smooth metal finish, and we might be more lucky there.

"When you've done that, Sergeant, come back here. Take a bus if you don't feel like a walk."

Adair turned back to Phoebe Wren. He saw a slightly-built girl of about twenty, with short brown hair. Not a beauty of the 'chocolate-box' variety, but stunningly attractive, nevertheless.

"Now, Miss, let's have our little chat. I understand that you prefer not to use your title?"

"That's right. It really is a nonsense. Hereditary titles like father's earldom were all very well back in the seventeenth century, but they are totally incongruous today.

"Courtesy titles like mine are even more illogical. My eldest brother takes one of father's subsidiary titles – Lord Hoxne – as a courtesy, but my younger brothers are mere honourables. Yet if father had ten daughters every one would be styled Lady. As it happens, I'm the only one, but that's irrelevant.

"It's also ludicrous that a woman marrying any titled man takes his title, whereas if I marry a commoner my husband gets nothing – it'll still be Lady Phoebe and Mr whatever.

"But in other ways there's a disgraceful bias against females. Evelyn was telling me last night that her father's title passed to her younger brother. And there's only a tiny handful of peerages which can pass down the female line.

"Anyway, as I think my title is absurd, I've chosen to ignore it.

"Sorry – on my high horse again! Please, ask your questions."

The DCI, who thought Phoebe had made a

number of incontrovertible points, smiled faintly.

"After dinner last night, describe your movements, please."

"We females left the men in the dining room. Several ladies went to the lavatory, but I thought I'd go back to the drawing room until the rush was over. I think all of them had come back after about ten minutes, so I left the room to go myself.

"As I was coming out of the lavatory I was accosted – that's the only appropriate word – by Jocelyn Hardingham.

"Let me go back a few hours. I don't know if Evelyn has explained this to you, but she invited both Jocelyn and me for one purpose only – to get us married to each other. I don't know if Jocelyn was aware of this matchmaking exercise, but I certainly wasn't – had I known I most certainly should not have come. Although I'd never met the man I'd heard of his reputation. I'd met Evelyn a couple of times at our house, but I'd never been here.

"When the invitation arrived, I just thought it would be an interesting experience to meet some of the people that I heard frequented Evelyn's gatherings.

"Anyway, as soon as I was introduced to Jocelyn, he monopolised me, first in the drawing room, and then at the dinner table – where inevitably I found myself seated next to him.

"Then, as I emerged from the lavatory after

dinner, he actually propositioned me – said he was retiring to bed immediately, and suggested I make some excuse and come to his room. He said he was in the Piccadilly Room, and he obviously knew that I was in the St George's Room, because he had the gall to say that I could easily slip back to my room next door before the maid brought the tea in the morning.

"I was so surprised – shocked, really – that I didn't speak at all; I just walked back to the drawing room and he followed.

"He then went off to bed as he had said he would. Whether he expected me to turn up in his room I'll never know.

"But whatever you may think, Chief Inspector, I didn't take up his offer."

"Tell us about everyone's movements after Hardingham had gone to bed, up to the time some of the guests departed."

"We sort of gathered into little groups around the room, sometimes sitting, sometimes standing. The groups were quite – what's the word? – fluid.

"Oh – you want to know who left the room after that and might have nipped upstairs and done the foul deed. Well, I did, for one. I don't know if it was the shock of being invited – without even a pretence of romance – to sleep with a man on the strength of a few hours' acquaintance, but my waterworks seemed to be working overtime. I was absent for probably five or six minutes –

enough time, I suppose, to have run upstairs and shot the man.

"I know Andrew Wymondham also left the room, because I was with him when he rather coarsely mentioned his own bladder problem. I can't say if anyone else went out – it's quite possible, and given the amount of drinking, even probable.

"When Evelyn's Doctor told us at breakfast what had happened, I wondered at first why I hadn't heard the shot. Now, it's clear that the wretched man was killed while the guests were in the drawing room – and that's much nearer the back of the house than the Piccadilly Room.

"Well, you can arrest me if you like, but it'll be a waste of your time. I can give you a *précis* of my defence now, if you like."

Adair laughed.

"No need, miss. You'll say that you had never met Hardingham before, and had no idea that he was going to offend you.

"You'll say that in any case being propositioned isn't even remotely a motive for murder.

"You'll say that you don't carry a pistol just in case you need to shoot someone who offends you.

"And perhaps the most persuasive argument of all is this. I understand you've been told that Hardingham was shot and fell to the floor. He was then picked up and lifted onto the bed. You'll say that you, as a very petite young lady, don't have the physical strength to lift a dead man of his weight.

"Or have I missed another crucial point?"

It was Phoebe's turn to laugh.

"No, Chief Inspector; you've covered the salient arguments for the defence."

"Thank you then, Miss Wren, that's all. You're free to leave the house when you like."

Phoebe grinned. "I'd like to stay for a while and see what happens – but as Evelyn's objective has failed so spectacularly, I may now be *persona non grata*. Good luck to you in your hunt anyway – Jocelyn was an obnoxious cad, but that doesn't mean he deserved the death penalty.

"Oh, and am I free to tell the others that the gun has been found?"

"Given that one of the maids saw its discovery, I think there would be little point in saying your fellow-guests are to be kept in the dark! Yes, go ahead and tell them."

CHAPTER 7

After the girl had gone, the DCI looked at Borthwick again.

"Well, Sergeant?"

"I don't know, sir. Your performance as defence counsel was very convincing. But on her own admission she was annoyed – and that showed on her face, as Mrs Wilcox observed.

"Then there's the fact that the pistol is tiny. I remember now that I've heard that women carry them as 'purse pistols' for self-defence. Perhaps not much in this country, but who knows?

"As for having the strength to lift the body, what if she had an accomplice?

"So I don't really doubt that you're right, sir, but I'm just not 100% sure. Sorry."

"Well done, Sergeant. Don't be sorry, they're all good points. I agree that we can't eliminate her just yet."

The study door opened, and Mrs Forbes-Kerr came in.

"Phoebe returned looking pleased, Chief Inspector, but she didn't ask anyone else to come and see you. I gather you have found the murder weapon, albeit not among someone's belongings. But can I deduce that you now know the culprit?"

"Alas no, ma'am. These things take time. It was something of a miracle that the pistol turned up, and it doesn't yet point us to any individual. But if you read detective stories, you'll know that it takes time to sort out motive, means, opportunity, and so on. Subject to the *post mortem* results, I'm confident that we have found the means. I'm also confident that we'll get the rest eventually."

"Good. You don't seem to have called for refreshments, and it is getting towards lunchtime now. Shall I order a selection of sandwiches and so on for you to eat in here?"

"That would be much appreciated, ma'am. While those are being prepared, could we see someone else? Lord Wymondham, perhaps, but anyone will do."

The hostess nodded, and left the room. Within five minutes, the Marquis appeared. He smiled affably as he took the chair the DCI indicated.

"Glad you found the pistol so soon," he remarked, "saved a lot of poking around in our personal belongings. Do you know whose it is?"

"Matter of fact, m'lord, I was wondering if it might be yours."

Wymondham guffawed loudly.

"'Fraid not, old boy. I have half a dozen shotguns at my country place, but I've never owned anything that wasn't smooth-bored. And I have no guns here in London anyway."

"Did you see war service?"

"In a sense. I joined the Yeomanry in 1899, and served for six years. I resigned – still a mere captain – when my father died and I came into the title.

"When war broke out, they seemed to welcome me back. But by 1914 I was nearly forty, and the powers that be wouldn't let me go overseas. So I spent the war years involved in staff work – training camps, supplies, and so on. A year into the war they pushed me up to major, and by the Armistice I'd made colonel.

"But how is that relevant, Chief Inspector? From what young Phoebe told us a few minutes ago, this pistol couldn't be a 'spoil of war' if manufacture wasn't started until the war had ended. So even if I'd been posted to some place where that sort of thing went on, I couldn't have got hold of it."

"It probably only relevant in the sense that the culprit almost certainly knows how to load and cock a semi-automatic pistol – which may mean army service."

The peer grunted. "Like all officers, I suppose, I was issued with a heavy service revolver. My batman cleaned it every week – although as I never fired it that must have been an easy task. I have never held an automatic pistol in my hand in all my life."

"Let's move on," said Adair. "Tell us about your movements between leaving the dining room and going to bed – and other people's movements as far as you know them."

"Mine are simple enough. I went to the lavatory after dinner. I then went into the drawing room, where over the next hour and a half or so I talked at various times to every other guest – including my wife. At about a quarter past eleven – can't be certain of the time – I went to the lavatory again. I suppose I was away for five minutes or so. No, I didn't go upstairs, and no, I didn't kill young Hardingham. Why on earth should I?"

"Did you know him?"

"Not really. I've known his father for years – we're more-or-less contemporaries, and often meet in the Lords. When Jocelyn was a boy, he came to my house with his parents a few times, and I saw him when I visited theirs. But until last night, it must be ten years since I'd last seen him. My own children are not much younger than him, but don't seem to move in the same circles – certainly they've never brought him to one of my houses as a guest. In fact I don't recall any of them mentioning him.

"That's odd, now I come to think about it, because on paper he must be classed as a very eligible bachelor. My twin daughters, only a year or so older than Phoebe Wren, seem to think of nothing but young males, but Hardingham doesn't seem to be in contention."

"Other people's movements, m'lord?"

"Sorry; yes. Can't say I would have noticed everyone's coming and going, don't you know, but I do know young Phoebe left the room, because I was sitting talking with her at the time. About ten past eleven, give or take a few minutes. But she was hardly away long enough to get up the stairs, let alone to kill Hardingham and put him to bed.

"Oh – it's just come back to me. Crampton left the room. I sort of noticed him out of the corner of my eye. He left by the door nearer the garden end of the room, not the usual one. I didn't notice him come back. I don't doubt that he killed lots of Germans during the war, but I can't believe he could be a murderer.

"Afraid I can't think of anyone else who went out."

"Well, thank you, m'lord. I have no more questions. Mrs Forbes-Kerr is sending us some food in here shortly, and no doubt you and the other guests will be taking lunch in the dining room. We don't want to disrupt that, but perhaps you would ask one of your fellow-guests to join us here as soon as may be convenient afterwards?"

"Of course, Chief Inspector. Leave it with me."

As Lord Wymondham left the room, Morgan arrived, followed by a footman pushing a trolley. A maid completed the procession.

"Some refreshments for you, gentlemen," said Morgan. There is a bottle of Muscadet – to go with the smoked salmon sandwiches.

Without being instructed, the junior staff started to transfer the food onto the desktop, and placed a clean plate and glass in front of each detective. The Butler deftly opened the bottle, and poured a little into the DCI's glass. Smiling to himself for the third time that morning, Adair sampled it and professed himself satisfied.

"We'll leave the trifle on the trolley, sir; perhaps you would help yourselves when you are ready. Would you prefer tea or coffee to finish?"

Both detectives chose tea, and Morgan said that it would be brought in twenty minutes. The tail-coated Butler then withdrew, shepherding the maid in her black outfit with starched white apron and frilly cap, and the footman in his smart yellow and black uniform, ahead of him.

"Gorgeous sandwiches, sir; looks like there's some egg mayonnaise ones as well as the salmon. Crusts all cut off, too. Never seen that before!

"Can't complain, Sergeant. Better than those in the Yard canteen, for sure."

He took a larger gulp of his wine. "Nice and dry," he remarked, and I bet this bottle cost a bob or two.

"Actually, on the rare occasions I have wine I prefer red – but if I'd asked for that with fish I think Morgan would have fainted in horror."

The two officers were silent for the next few minutes. After sating themselves on sandwiches, they both eyed the delicious-looking trifle, wondering if they could squeeze some in.

"Perhaps we could ask for that to be left in the room when they come to clear away," suggested Borthwick. "I might manage a portion in half an hour or so."

"I'm with you there, Sergeant – excellent idea. Now, what do you think so far?"

"I don't think it was Lord Wymondham, sir. I've only met three murderers, so I haven't much experience, but he doesn't come across as a killer to me. And he made a good point about the gun.

"But this man Crampton. Do you think he sneaked out to avoid anyone noticing?"

"Could be. Mrs Forbes-Kerr told me Crampton had a very distinguished war record. He was decorated for gallantry, so he didn't spend the war in a cushy billet. Must be able to handle a pistol. But we're back to the same old problem – motive."

The two men were contemplating this when a different maid returned with yet another trolley. Giving a quick curtsey, she gave each man a cup and saucer, and his own teapot, milk jug, and sugar bowl.

She started to clear away the lunch things, when Adair told her to leave the trifle and plates and spoons. She grinned at this, and transferred the trifle paraphernalia onto the desk.

"Cook makes a lovely trifle, sirs," she remarked. "Shall I pour the tea?" Adair shook his head, and the girl left, pushing one of the trolleys.

The men poured the tea, and the DCI was about to speak again when there was a tap on the door and another guest came into the study.

"'Afternoon, gentlemen," said the newcomer, "I'm Travis Egerton.

"Hope I'm not too early, but I should like to go and make some calls if you release me, so I skipped the dessert course. I see you haven't had yours yet, either!"

"Please take a seat, sir. This is Detective Sergeant Borthwick.

As the men shook hands, Borthwick tried hard not to stare at the huge incongruous moustache on the sixty-something-year-old face under the bald skull.

"You've probably heard about the questions we're asking, sir," said Adair, "so do you want to kick off?"

Egerton laughed.

"Saves you the bother of asking, I suppose – well of course.

"First, I didn't know Hardingham at all. Never met him, to my knowledge, although I come across his father from time to time.

"Second, I possess a pistol. It's a point three-two Smith & Wesson hammerless, with a short barrel. I have a licence for it in this country – personally approved by your Commissioner, in fact – and I carry it in an underarm holster here and especially abroad. Self-defence, you know – there have been two attempts to kidnap me over the last few years. It's in my room now, if you want to see it, but I gather you have already found the pistol that killed Hardingham.

"Third, I was in the drawing room when Hardingham said goodnight, and I didn't leave the room again until those of us who were still in the house all retired to bed – about half past midnight. There must be others who can vouch for the fact that I didn't get up from my comfortable armchair.

"So I plead not guilty."

"Your plea is noted, sir. What about the movements of other guests?"

"I had my back to the doors, and I spent the best part of two hours having interesting conversations with those in the chair and on the sofa near me. The occupants of those changed three or four times, but someone always came to keep me amused. But I'm afraid I didn't see who left the room at any time.

I can tell you something else, though. In the little group of chairs nearest to me, the Eastons and the Routledges were together all the time. I am absolutely certain that none of the four left the room between Hardingham going to bed, and them standing up to go home. Other people came and spoke to them from time to time, but they never rose from their chairs.

"Thank you sir. I note your familiarity with revolvers, but what about automatic pistols – did you serve in the war?"

Egerton hesitated.

"I did, yes, although I can't go into detail. I was involved in, shall we say, intelligence work. And yes, I carried an automatic pistol throughout the war, and had to use it on occasion."

There was a silence for a few seconds, before Egerton spoke again.

"You probably don't want to discuss the case with a suspect, Chief Inspector, but how do you account for this business of putting the man in his bed after he was shot?"

Adair shrugged his shoulders. "A complete mystery. To delay discovery should someone happen to come into the room perhaps.

"Anyway, thank you sir – you are of course free to leave the house. If the others have finished lunch, perhaps you would invite one of them to join us?"

"Can't be him, sir" observed Borthwick after the door closed.

"It would seem not. Interesting and probably highly dangerous war though – the sort of man who was probably trained to kill people silently, I guess. Certainly I don't think he'd baulk at killing someone if it became necessary. But we'll have to keep looking.

"Looks as though the four guests who went home are out of the picture, though.

"You haven't seen the elderly lady, Mrs Fitzwallace, Borthwick, but I can tell you that she is about ninety, and although I haven't seen her standing up I guess she's very small. No way on earth could she have lifted Hardingham's body. We'll have to eliminate her too.

"The business of putting Hardingham in the bed, sir. Could it be in case the Wren girl came into the room?"

"I think not. That would mean that the killer overheard Hardingham's invitation, which seems unlikely. And even if he did hear it, he couldn't know how long it would be before she arrived. So he couldn't afford to mess about because he might be caught red-handed. If he expected a visitor in the room, he – or she – would want to get out as fast as possible.

"Also, suppose she did turn up. Surely she would expect movement from her beau, and notice pretty quickly that he was dead?"

Borthwick nodded sadly. Before either man could speak again, a tap on the door presaged the arrival of the next guest.

CHAPTER 8

There being only one remaining male guest in the house, the Yard officers deduced the identity of this one before the man introduced himself.

"I'm Patrick Crampton," he announced, sitting down unbidden in the chair opposite the DCI.

"I appreciate you have your job to do, Chief Inspector, and I can't deny that it looks black for one of my fellow-guests, but I still can't believe one of them did it. For the avoidance of doubt, I didn't kill the man.

"Anyway, I'll cut to the chase. I didn't know Hardingham at all. I was introduced to him before dinner, and spoke to him briefly for a few minutes. He seemed a personable young man. I didn't sit near him at dinner, and in fact he seemed engrossed in the girl beside him. I didn't speak to him again, as he had no sooner arrived in the drawing room after the meal than he asked to be excused, and went off to bed.

"I had no reason to kill the man."

"I understand you were in the army during

the war, sir. Will you give us a brief outline?"

"Can't see what this has to do with the case. Anyway, yes, I joined up in 1915 and was commissioned shortly afterwards. I served in France and Belgium, and for a short time in Palestine. I was demobbed as a substantive major, acting half-colonel."

"You carried a sidearm, of course. Are you familiar with automatic pistols?"

"I am. I used a Colt automatic in preference to the standard service revolver. And I shot a number of people, without doubt. But I did not shoot Hardingham. Why the hell would I want to do that?"

"Why would anyone want to shoot him, sir? But someone, for some reason, did."

Crampton grunted. "True."

"Did you leave the drawing room for any reason between the time Mr Hardingham went to bed, and the time a few of the guests went home?"

"Matter of fact I did, yes. I needed a pee. I hadn't gone when we men first left the dining room, but needed to go perhaps twenty minutes later – about eleven o'clock, I suppose.

"But no, I wasn't out of the room for more than a few minutes. Certainly not time enough to dash upstairs, shoot Hardingham, put him to bed, and rush downstairs again – and that's without the necessity of using the lavatory as well."

"Why did you leave the drawing room by the second door, sir?"

"Second door? Oh I see what you mean. I was standing by the doors into the garden. There was nobody with me at the time, and I was looking out – Evelyn had electric lights set up around her flower beds and so on. The need to relieve myself came on, so I naturally left the room by the nearest door. Nothing sinister about it – it opens into the same corridor as the other door. I returned by the usual door anyway, as it's nearer to the lavatory."

"Very good, thank you sir. No reason to detain you in the house any longer."

"All right; thank you. Can I summon anyone else to see you?"

"Lady Wymondham, if it's convenient for her now; thank you sir."

The arrival of the Marchioness at the study door coincided with the return of Sergeant Gemmill, who was being escorted by a footman.

"Good afternoon, m'lady," greeted Adair. "Please take a seat.

"Sergeant, just sit down in the corner – I won't be more than a few minutes with her ladyship."

Elizabeth Fox-Gilbert had a pedigree even longer than the lengthy one boasted by her husband, being the daughter of the Earl of Penrith – himself the sixteenth holder of that title. Nobody talking to her, however, would have guessed at any such background. She came across as distinctly middle-class – perhaps a nurse or (if she hadn't been married) a primary school teacher. She had, like Mrs Wilcox, spent much of the war as a FANY, and France had awarded her the *Croix de Guerre* – a rare honour. The detectives would never be aware of this.

She smiled at the two men as Adair introduced his colleague.

"Andrew and the others have told me of your interrogation procedure, Chief Inspector. I understand there are no thumbscrews or rubber truncheons employed!"

Both officers grinned.

"No, m'lady. Frowned upon, these days.

"Your husband said that he knew Mr Hardingham years ago, when he was a boy, but hadn't seen him for years. Is that also the case with you?"

"It is, yes. I hadn't seen Jocelyn since he was about seventeen or eighteen, while he was still at Harrow. But let me come back to that later, if I may, after you've asked your other questions."

"Very well. Can you handle a pistol?"

"To be honest, I've never tried. I'm pretty good with a shotgun – I have a pair of bespoke Boss twelve-bores. So if a pistol was put into my hand, I guess I could soon learn to use it."

"As I'm sure you've gathered, Mr Hardingham was probably shot before everyone went to bed – in fact almost certainly before the guests who were not staying overnight left the house. What can you tell us about people's movements between the time Mr Hardingham retired and the time people started to leave?"

"Yes, I understand. Well, I can say who definitely didn't leave the room at any time. They were the Eastons, the Routledges, Ada Fitzwallace, Travis Egerton, Evelyn, and me.

"I can also say that my husband left the room, as did Phoebe Wren. I didn't actually see Patrick Crampton leave the room, but I did see him return. I can't tell you about Ralph Blanchflower – he was out of my eye line for much of the time.

"Does that help, Chief Inspector?"

"Yes, m'lady, in that it confirms what others have said.

"Now, you were going to tell us something else?"

"Yes. When Andrew came back from talking to you, he remarked that our two daughters had never mentioned Jocelyn, and on reflection he found that a bit strange, as they do spend a lot of time even in our hearing discussing the relative merits of various eligible males. And Jocelyn was, at least on paper, about as eligible a bachelor as could be found anywhere.

"When he said that I suddenly recalled something I heard a year or so ago. I emphasise that this is hearsay, and may be totally irrelevant.

"Amelia and Ariadne were talking together in our drawing room – a Sunday afternoon, I think it was. I was present, reading a newspaper or something, and not involved in their chatter at all. They were discussing men. I didn't even listen to most of their conversation, but one thing did sink in. Ariadne said something on the lines of 'sowing his wild oats is one thing, but Jocelyn's gone much too far this time', and her sister replied 'yes, we should have nothing more to do with him'.

"I didn't take a lot of notice – I assumed they were talking about Jocelyn Hardingham, and thought he'd probably been trying to take more liberties with one or both of them than they would accept. I never thought any more about it until just now.

"But it seems to me that Jocelyn's character must be relevant here, so I thought I should tell you."

"Thank you. Yes, we'll be looking into his character. I wonder if you would ask your daughters, delicately of course, exactly what it was that made them decide to cut him?"

"I'll do that, Chief Inspector, but they're both away until tomorrow at the earliest, and I can't get hold of them until they get back home. I'll contact you at Scotland Yard if I find out anything."

"Thank you, m'lady; I understand you are staying here for another night anyway, but you are free to leave whenever you wish."

All three detectives stood as the Marchioness left the study.

CHAPTER 9

The telephone had rung several times during the various interviews, and Adair had ignored it. It rang again as the DCI turned to Gemmill.

"Any news, Sergeant?"

"No good news sir. Mr Brough unloaded the pistol, and I checked for prints. None on the gun itself, and none on the magazine either. Completely wiped clean.

"He showed me his, er, Liliput, and I could see what you meant about his one having the smarter finish. He showed me what he said was a typical modern automatic, a point three-eight Colt, and that really showed how tiny ours was.

"Mr Brough also mentioned that around 45,000 of these pistols were produced, although he thinks very few would have come into this country."

"Ah well, I didn't have high hopes. Too many criminals have heard about fingerprints these days."

There was a knock on the door, and a footman appeared.

"There is a telephone call for you, Chief

Inspector. If you just pick up the instrument here, I'll replace the one in the hall."

Adair picked up the handset.

"Just hang on a moment," he said, waiting until he heard the sound of the other receiver being put down.

"Hallo; DCI Adair here...Yes...Good, that narrows it down a bit, although we're getting nowhere near finding a motive yet...We have the gun, by the way, so your bullet matches...Yes...To the Yard, please...Thanks Tim, be seeing you.' Bye.

"The Pathologist confirms that death occurred sometime between ten and eleven thirty. God knows how they work that sort of thing out. Anyway, we know that Hardingham was still alive at about half past ten, so the range is now actually quite small, and all the guests were still present in the house.

"The bullet is distorted, of course, but the Doc thinks it was a point two-five. That's 6.35 mm.

"But going back to the guests. Most are already eliminated from the list of suspects, and really only Crampton, Lord Wymondham, and the Wren girl still remain under starter's orders. We can ask more detailed questions about the length of time each of those was out of the room, but frankly I can't see how any of them could have had enough time to do what we know was done.

"And we're still lacking any sort of credible motive. Phoebe Wren is the only one with any sort of motive, and that one isn't remotely valid.

If I arrested and charged her now, no magistrate would even commit her for trial.

"Thoughts?"

"The lady who was here just now – is it lady Wymondham? – seemed to be implying that Hardingham was a bad lot, sir," said Gemmill, "and that he did something to one or both of her daughters. Could that be a motive for her husband? Or perhaps this other man Crampton has a daughter?"

"You mean Lord Wymondham was feigning his lack of knowledge about why the daughters never invited Hardingham to his house? It's a valid theory, Sergeant," replied the DCI, "and we'll check on Crampton's family as well.

"But if adverse things were known about this man – and it seems to date back a year or so at least – it seems odd for Mrs Forbes-Kerr to invite him specifically to meet a very young and impressionable girl. To act as a marriage broker, in fact. I need another word with her.

"Borthwick has been with me for all the interviews so far, Gemmill, so you can accompany me to see Lord and Lady Hardingham. Today, if possible.

"While we're doing that, I want you, Borthwick, to go and see Sir Oliver and Lady Easton, and Mr and Mrs Routledge. We'll get the addresses from Mrs F. Better telephone first to make an appointment. It seems the four of them are in the clear as far as the murder is concerned, but it's worthwhile seeing what they remember about the movements of others – particularly how long Crampton, Wymondham, and Wren were out of the room. They probably won't remember – may not have even noticed – but we must check.

"That leaves Mrs Fitzwallace, and she might be offended if we ignore her. So you and I will see her, Gemmill, before we go to the Hardinghams. Perhaps we'll have a chat with the hostess at the same time."

He stood up, and pressed the bellpush. Within a minute, the Butler appeared.

To Adair's secret delight, as he expected Morgan intoned the classic words.

"You rang, sir?"

"Please find your mistress, Morgan, and ask her two things.

First, could she please provide us with the addresses and telephone numbers for Lord Hardingham, the Eastons, and the Routledges?

"Second, if it is convenient, could she and Mrs Fitzwallace join us in here for a few minutes?"

The Butler gave another almost imperceptible bow, and left the room.

Within five minutes, the study door opened again, and the two ladies came in, Mrs Forbes-Kerr holding what was clearly an address book.

"This is Ada Fitzwallace, gentlemen," she announced.

Adair introduced his two sergeants. Gemmill now sat at the desk beside the DCI, and the two women opposite. Borthwick remained standing, anticipating that he would be leaving once in possession of the addresses.

I have the details you want, Chief Inspector – do you want to write them down?"

"If you please, ma'am. Borthwick, you note your two, and Gemmill you take down Lord Hardingham's."

This exercise took only two minutes, and the officers immediately realised that all three addresses were close by in Mayfair.

"It would, I think, be courteous if my Sergeant calls ahead, ma'am. Will it be all right if he uses the telephone in the hall?"

The hostess nodded. "Yes, of course. But when you asked for the details, I telephoned Edwin Hardingham; he is at home and expecting a visit. I haven't spoken to the others."

"Thank you, ma'am. Right, Borthwick, off you go," instructed the DCI. "You can walk to both these houses, assuming you find at least one of the residents at home in each. When you've finished, go back to the Yard, and we'll meet there."

He turned back to the interviewees.

"Apologies, ladies; I won't keep you very long."

"No need to apologise," said Mrs Fitzwallace, who might be nearer ninety than eighty but whose facial expression suggested a woman who was not only *compos mentis* but was also highly intelligent. Her eyes twinkled as she added, "I just wonder why you think that I, alone among the guests here, require a chaperone for this interview?"

Adair smiled.

"Such a thing never entered my mind, ma'am. The fact is that other witnesses have said that you never left the drawing room during the crucial period, and so are not a suspect. I just want to ask what you may remember about that evening – and in particular about the movement of others. As I also had a couple of questions for your sister-in-law, I thought it would be convenient to see you both together."

"I see." She laughed. "When a beautiful young thing like Lady Phoebe was allowed to come in alone, but I wasn't, I couldn't help wondering!

"Anyway, you want to know what I recall of the evening between Jocelyn retiring to bed and some of the guests leaving to go home. Well, I may be very old, but my eyes are still sharp, and my memory is very good. In the drawing room I was seated on an upright chair facing the doors. I find it difficult to get up from armchairs and settees. Various people came and talked to me, but my view of the doors was never obstructed for more than a second or so.

"Phoebe left the room first, not long after Jocelyn went to bed. She was away for seven or eight minutes. Not long after that, Patrick Crampton went out through the door at the garden end of the room. He was away for even less time – five minutes or so. A bit later, Andrew and

Phoebe were both standing beside me, and Andrew suddenly said 'Excuse me, weak bladder, must go'. He was only away for five or six minutes.

"Nobody else left the room, although Morgan and two of the maids were coming and going, of course.

"Does that help, Chief Inspector?"

"It confirms what everyone else has told us, ma'am; thank you.

"Now, how well did you know Mr Hardingham?"

"I didn't know him at all. I rarely come to town – indeed for many years I've avoided doing so. My husband died before the war, but even before he passed on, both of us preferred to stay in the country. I married not long after 'coming out', and since then my interest has been in County society, rather than in London society. I leave that sort of thing to Evelyn! I gather several of last night's guests were acquainted with the dead man's father, but as far as I know I have never had that pleasure. I've heard of him, but was unaware of what offspring he might have."

"Thank you, ma'am," said Adair, thinking that sixty years ago this lady must have been not only a beauty but a wonderful companion for her lucky husband.

"If I may turn to you now, ma'am," he continued, looking at Mrs Forbes-Kerr. "A delicate matter."

The DCI thought that Mrs Fitzwallace's

expression became even more alert, as though she was anticipating some scandal, and for all her alleged disinterest in London society would take pleasure in hearing about it.

"When you first spoke to me, ma'am, you explained why you had invited Mr Hardingham – and indeed the young lady. You mentioned that he liked to 'play the field', to use your own expression. We have learned, from different sources, that there may be a bit more to it than that.

"One of your guests described him as 'totally amoral'. Another said that certain girls would no longer have anything to do with him.

"I have to ask, ma'am, if you were aware of that reputation before suggesting him as a match for the granddaughter of a close friend?"

"*Mea culpa*, Chief Inspector. Ada says I involve myself in the affairs of London society, and of course that is correct. As you probably know, there are half a dozen women like me – Emerald Cunard, Laura Corrigan, Margaret Greville, and a couple of others – whose whole lives revolve around the doings of those who are rich, powerful, or influential.

"But I fear that we all have one weakness. The people we socialise with are those who are either already at the top of their tree, or are rising fast towards that position. So, very few are under thirty years of age, and most are above forty.

"That means, alas, that I rarely meet young people – let alone listen to their views, news and gossip.

"So no, I had absolutely no idea that Jocelyn was as you describe him. I have spoken to a couple of people on the telephone today, and I now belatedly learn that he was apparently the worst kind of philanderer. I am so thankful that Phoebe saw fit to rebuff the advances she tells me he made last night.

"That said, I certainly wouldn't have wished him dead."

The four sat in silence for a full minute.

"I'm going to break a confidence now, Chief Inspector, and I trust this will go no further.

"When I told Edwin of his son's death, he said something which at the time I thought was odd. Now, not so much.

"He said, 'God moves in a mysterious way; in this instance perhaps he does know what is best'."

There was another silence, as this information was absorbed.

"A further delicate question, ladies," said Adair at last.

"Can either of you think of any female relative of any of the guests here last night, who might have been the subject of Mr Hardingham's attentions?"

The two ladies looked at each other. "No use asking me," said Mrs Fitzwallace, "I hardly knew anyone here. And I have sons and grandsons, but alas no granddaughters. I do have a great-granddaughter, but as she is only four it'll hopefully be many years before she needs to be warned about the likes of young Hardingham."

"Andrew and Elizabeth have daughters, and so does Esmeralda," said Evelyn. "I rather think Patrick has a daughter too. The Eastons only have a son, and the Routledges are childless. Both Travis and Ralph are confirmed bachelors."

"Thank you. Informative but not, alas, light-shedding. Thank you also for the food, ma'am – it was much appreciated. We'll be off now, and leave you in peace. However, I fear we may need to disturb you again tomorrow."

"Just one last thing, Chief Inspector. I have instructed my servants not to speak about this incident outside the house – and indeed, not to speculate about it at all. None of my guests would dream of speaking to the newspapers – not even Ralph, who works for one. Do the police report this sort of thing to the Press?"

"Certainly not, ma'am. But leaks do occur. The ambulance men who took Mr Hardingham away – they would know that this is an unusually prestigious address for them to collect a murder victim, and might well talk. Or a mortuary attendant would inevitably see the name tag which may well have had 'the Honourable' on it. Even the Pathologist conducting the autopsy might discuss the case with his colleagues – no reason why he shouldn't – and the news spreads that way. Eventually, the Press gets to learn of most murders."

CHAPTER 10

The Hardingham residence was in Curzon Street, not four hundred yards away, so Adair told Gemmill that they would leave the car where it was, and walk. Five minutes later, the DCI was pulling on a bell handle.

Mayfair was of course a very affluent neighbourhood, and the house was, by most standards, large. However, it did not come anywhere close to the size of Mrs Forbes-Kerr's property.

The door was answered by a diminutive maid, dressed identically to those in Douglas House – black dress, with starched white apron and cap. She bobbed a brief curtsey to the policemen.

"You'll be the detectives from Scotland Yard, sirs, I expect. 'Tis a terrible thing, to be sure. His Lordship has said to bring you to the study. May I have your names and ranks, please?"

The girl could be heard quietly repeating this information to herself, as she led them along a corridor. Reaching one of several solid oak doors, she tapped on it and opened it immediately. She stepped in and stood aside.

"Chief Inspector Adair and Sergeant Gemmill, m'lord."

"Thank you, Eunice," said the occupant of the room, rising from behind a large yew desk. That will be all.

"I'm Edwin Hardingham, gentlemen. Welcome. Not a happy time, but please dispense with any condolences."

He shook hands with both men, and waved them to chairs in front of the desk. They saw a slim man, just on the right side of sixty, of average height, with grey hair cut *en brosse*, and wearing tortoiseshell-framed spectacles.

"Apologies – before the maid left I should have offered you refreshments. Would you care for tea or something?"

"No thank you, m'lord; we don't expect to disturb you for long."

"I should explain that Merle, my wife, is not at home," the Viscount continued. She has gone to visit our remaining son in Cambridge. Although the university is down at present, Inigo has a little house in the city and remains there during some of his vacations.

"Now, I'm obviously happy to help, but first I'd be obliged if you would just give me the blunt facts – Evelyn didn't give me anything more than the fact that Jocelyn had been killed."

"As you wish, m'lord. Your son retired very

early, soon after dinner in fact, stating that he was tired. Not long after going up to his room, and before completely removing his dinner clothes, he was shot in the back of the head. Death would have been instantaneous. Then, for reasons which we don't understand, he was picked up from the floor, placed on the bed, and covered as if he were simply sleeping.

"The weapon has been found, hidden elsewhere in the house. It is a Liliput semi-automatic pistol. As yet we do not know where this came from.

"I have to ask if it could be your son's property – perhaps borrowed from a collection of yours?"

The peer shook his head. "I don't have a country house, and when I'm invited to stay with someone who has a shooting estate, I borrow a shotgun from my host. So I don't even own a shotgun, let alone a pistol.

"I can't say with certainty that Jocelyn never had such a thing, but if he did he didn't mention it in my hearing. Doesn't seem very likely that he'd be shot with his own pistol, though. If someone chose to go up to his bedroom in order to murder him, surely they wouldn't expect to find the weapon ready for them to use?

"I assume you believe that one of his fellow guests bore him a grudge?"

"I can't discuss our investigation in detail, m'lord. But I can say that we are looking into a possible motive – and in doing so the character of the victim has come into focus."

The DCI stopped, and looked meaningfully at the peer.

Hardingham groaned audibly.

"Oh God – you'll be alluding to Jocelyn's womanising. If all this comes out, as I suppose it will, it'll mean obloquy for Jocelyn in his grave, and scandal for the remaining family."

He shook his head sadly. "No doubt he was shot by someone whose daughter – or even wife – he seduced."

"Tell us something of his history in this respect, m'lord."

"He was at Harrow – followed in my footsteps, in fact. Now, at Harrow some boys turn out homosexual. Jocelyn certainly did not. He was very nearly expelled in his last year, for having an affair with a matron – who was some ten years older than he was, and by all accounts unattractive. The Head told me that there had been allegations of an earlier affair, one with a waitress from a café in the town. He was only reprieved because it was so close to the time for public examinations, and he was allowed to stay to take those, and left immediately after the last.

"He then went up to Oxford. There, and indeed over the eight or nine years since he came down, there have been many, many women. And of course I can only know of a proportion of those who no doubt existed.

"Some of those I know about – and I've met a number of them over the years – have been eminently suitable as girlfriends. I hear of others who are less so.

"It pains me to admit this, but I am aware that he has fathered two children out of wedlock. Neither of the mothers could be classed as society women, to say the least. I paid a large sum of money to each of them, making it clear it was a one-off payment, and I should never ever pay anything further.

"There may be more cases."

A possible new interpretation of something he had been told at Douglas House suddenly came into Adair's mind.

"I understand you sent your son abroad a year or two ago – was that connected with his, er, proclivities?"

"Oh, God," muttered the peer again. "Yes, it was. In January or February of last year he came to me with a story of yet another unwanted pregnancy. This time I gave him money, whereas previously I had personally negotiated with the women concerned. What I hadn't counted on – hadn't even considered – was the possibility that the girl might get a back-street abortion. Whether Jocelyn encouraged her in that I don't know. He denied it when he confessed to me a month or so later about what had happened. But anyway, the girl died soon after the process. The abortionist was never found, and the death was never connected to Jocelyn.

"But it was the last straw for me. I actually considered applying for a Reception Order under the 1890 Lunacy Act. I was only deterred from doing so by the fact that I should have had to testify to the facts in front of two doctors and a magistrate.

"So, I talked to an acquaintance who owns tea plantations in Ceylon. I admit that I didn't give him the whole story – just implied that I wanted to get my son away from a particular woman for a while. Anyway, it was agreed that he would go and learn how to run a tea plantation. I gave Jocelyn no choice – it was that, or I would stop his allowance and have him committed to a mental hospital.

"He had been out in Ceylon for a year when I heard that he was up to his old tricks. He was effectively openly cohabiting with a young native girl – not the done thing – and he was simultaneously engaged in a torrid affair with the wife of one of the English supervisors.

"It was my turn to be given no choice – my acquaintance told me Jocelyn was no longer welcome on the estate. I was obliged to ship him home. He returned about three months ago.

"I hold the lease on a small house in town, and Jocelyn has lived there rather than in this house since he came down from Oxford. He had lived there for seven or eight years. When he returned from Ceylon he just moved back into the house – I hadn't sub-let it while he was abroad –

and he promised to behave. It would appear that he has not kept that undertaking."

Hardingham fell silent, and sat staring down at the desk.

"Well, m'lord, I think you are perhaps being unduly pessimistic about the publicity," said Adair. "Fairly soon there will be an inquest into his death, and hopefully his murderer will eventually be brought to trial. It seems to me that the only matter which need concern either inquest or trial will be one specific instance of his philandering. Perhaps the public learning of one case – however unpleasant and however damaging to his own memory – wouldn't particularly affect your family's standing.

"I can assure you that the police are only interested in catching a killer – not in broadcasting lurid reports of your son's earlier behaviour. The only risk is really if some unscrupulous reporter starts to dig.

"I should add that it isn't even certain yet that your son's murder is connected with his treatment of some woman."

"Thank you, Chief Inspector. I appreciate your saying all that.

"You'll want to know about his conduct since his return, but I know absolutely nothing. I never visited his house in the three months he has been back, and although he has been here several times to see his mother and me, he didn't bring any female with him – nor did he even mention one as

I recall."

"I see. We have a set of keys, and presumably they are for the property. Do you have a set yourself?"

"Yes; I'm the leaseholder and pay all the charges. You'll be going in there to search for anything that might help, I assume? If so, I'd appreciate it if you would return that set of keys to me."

"Of course, m'lord. Can you give us the address, please?"

Hardingham gave an address in Moreton Terrace, which Gemmill noted in his pocketbook.

"Are there servants – did he employ a valet, for instance?"

"No; he lived alone – apart presumably from the occasional lady friend. I believe he had a char of some sort on an *ad hoc* basis, but I didn't interfere or enquire how he ran the house."

"Just one final matter, m'lord. In any case of murder, we have to consider who benefits, financially and otherwise. Do you know if Jocelyn made a will?"

"I'd be very surprised if he did, as he had no assets to speak of. He lived on a handsome allowance from me. The house wasn't his. I can't think that he had accumulated much in the way of savings."

Adair glanced at Gemmill to see if he wanted to ask anything, and received a quick shake of the head.

"That's it, m'lord, for the present anyway. The Coroner's Officer will be in contact should you be required at the inquest, although at present I don't see why you would be called to give evidence. We'll get along now." He and Gemmill rose.

"Just one further thing," said the peer as he also stood up. "I could of course ask Evelyn, but it may be that she would prevaricate. Do you know why she invited Jocelyn – not just to dinner, but to stay overnight? There is absolutely no way that he complied with her usual criteria for selecting guests."

The DCI hesitated. The truth would not put Mrs Forbes-Kerr in a positive light, even though her ignorance of the youth's track record was hardly her fault. Nor would Lord Hardingham look good as it might appear that he had concealed key facts from his friend. However, Adair could see no alternative, and briefly explained the matchmaking attempt.

"Oh God," muttered Hardingham for the third time. "What a mess. I know young Phoebe's father well – I suppose I'd better apologise to him."

"May I suggest that you don't rush into that, m'lord? Young people don't always tell their parents everything these days – as you yourself have just demonstrated. It may be that Lady Phoebe hasn't told her father anything about the improper proposal. And the fact that Mrs Forbes-Kerr was attempting to link two ostensibly well-matched members of the aristocracy is hardly a matter for which you need apologise."

"The peer nodded. "Yes, of course. Thank you again."

Hardingham saw the officers to the front door himself, and the two walked back to collect the car from Douglas House, Adair deeming Pimlico too far to travel on foot.

CHAPTER 11

Both officers knew the rough location of Moreton Street, but Gemmill had to consult the street map in the police car to ensure that Moreton Terrace was close by. He found that it was – together with Moreton Place and Moreton Close!

The properties here were comparatively narrow compared to Lord Hardingham's, and tiny compared to Mrs Forbes-Kerr's. However, they exuded affluence, having a lower ground floor, a ground floor accessed by steps, and two further floors. A 'Juliet' balcony with decorated iron railings graced each of the front windows on the first floor.

Gemmill parked the car almost directly outside, and the detectives walked up the short set of steps, Adair pulling out the keys he had collected from Hardingham's bedroom. The door opened without difficulty.

Inside, the property was not so well maintained as the exterior. There was dust on the hall table, and it looked as though the 'char' mentioned by Lord Hardingham was either inefficient or had not put in a recent appearance.

Adair looked into what was clearly the main living room – well-furnished but again in need of a clean. Spotting an open roll-top bureau against one wall, he issued instructions.

"I'll go through this desk, Sergeant; chances are all his papers are here. You look over the rest of the house."

Sitting on the swivel chair, the DCI started to look through the papers in the pigeon holes. He found nothing of interest – only a few bills and receipts. Pulling open the main drawer, he found three leather-bound three-year diaries , and he took these out and began to look through one. Almost immediately he stopped, realising that this one covered a period some years before. He quickly found the most recent, which was almost full.

The first diary dated back to the time when young Hardingham was probably halfway through his sojourn at Oxford, and the final entry in the most recent volume was made only three days ago.

Practically every entry was made up only of a single female Christian name. A very few included a surname as well. Some names appeared regularly over a period of weeks; others had only a single entry and never came up again. But even in the cases where some girl seemed be a fixture for a month or so, one or more other names usually appeared in the middle of the sequence.

Adair whistled to himself as he saw the

extent of what he could only presume to be young Hardingham's conquests.

He scanned the more recent entries, but could see that identifying most would be almost impossible.

He sat silently for several minutes, staring at – but not seeing – an elegant grandmother clock that was still ticking away, unaware that its master would never come to wind it again.

Gemmill came into the room, and seeing the DCI apparently in a trance, sat down without speaking. He was accustomed to his boss's habit, and knew that these sessions quite often produced useful ideas.

After a couple more minutes, Adair stirred again, and seeing Gemmill sitting across the room, apologised.

"Find anything, Sergeant?"

"Nothing of interest, sir."

"Well, I've found some diaries. If each of the several hundred female names represents a conquest, all I can say is that Hardingham makes Don Juan look like the male equivalent of a nun. Unfortunately, almost all the names lack a surname. We'll try to identify some of the more recent ones, but it's going to be a difficult and quite possibly thankless task."

Adair tucked the three diaries in the briefcase he always carried, and stood up.

"Let's get back."

It was just after four-thirty when they

reached Scotland Yard, and Adair asked the desk officer if Sergeant Borthwick had returned. It seemed he was still out.

"Tell him to come straight up to my office when he comes in."

In fact, Gemmill and Adair had hardly sat down when Borthwick arrived.

"Excellent timing; let's see if my Secretary can get us a cup of tea before she goes home. He stood up, stuck his head into the adjoining office, and issued instructions. Sitting down again, he looked at Borthwick.

"Right, what did you learn from the Eastons and the Routledges."

"Nice people, all four of them. No trace of 'we are quality, you are scum', which I'd sort of half expected. They were only just coming to terms with the fact they'd been in a house when a murder was committed.

"Anyway, their stories back up all the others. None of the four left the drawing room between dinner and going home. They couldn't all swear to the same things, but between them it was confirmed that nobody other than Wren, Crampton, and Wymondham left the room. Those who observed those movements thought that none was away for more than seven or eight minutes, if that."

"All right. Gemmill, tell Borthwick what we heard from Lord Hardingham."

Gemmill gave his fellow-sergeant an

accurate précis of the interview with the Viscount. Adair followed with an outline of what was – and what wasn't – in the diaries.

"When I first spoke to Mrs Forbes-Kerr, she actually stated that the murderer must be one of her guests, as none of her servants had ever met Jocelyn Hardingham. I thought exactly the same. But then two further things arose to suggest that idea may – only may – be wrong.

"First, it turned out that most of the guests didn't know Hardingham either – and those that did hadn't actually seen him for years.

"Second, the timing of the murder is such that it seems to be very tricky for any of the guests to have done it.

"So, I think we have to consider the staff after all. Remiss of me not to have included them in the initial interviews anyway."

"Tasks for tomorrow. I have the Christian names of the Douglas House females." The DCI slid Mrs Forbes-Kerr's list across the desk. Borthwick, you go through the most recent diary. That starts about a year before Hardingham went to Ceylon, so that's the time to begin. Check the names of staff against the names in the diary. You'll need some sort of system. It may be best to get my Secretary to go through the diary first, and produce a typed list. Ah, here she is."

Mrs Haskell came in, bearing a tray on which were three cups of tea and a plate of biscuits.

"Thank you," said Adair. "We're just

debating how best to check names on a short list against perhaps a hundred names in a diary. Here, look."

He opened a diary to show how the names were entered.

"I could go through the diary, and type out a simple list, sir. It would be far easier to cross-check one list with the other, rather than turning pages all the time. Then I can work in conjunction with you or one of your sergeants. He calls out the names and I type them, and then we take a list each and the one with the longer list calls out each name in turn. It'll be much quicker with two people."

"Excellent. I need to lock these diaries up tonight, but first thing in the morning I'd like you to take this one and make a list from it. You and Sergeant Borthwick can then do the checking. Get off home now."

"The names of the staff on the list here – Eileen, Dorcas, Niamh, Florence, Estelle, Bernice. We'd better add Ariadne and Amelia, the daughters of Lord Wymondham.

"Who else, gentlemen?"

Mrs F said she thought Mr Crampton may have a daughter, sir," offered Gemmill, "and he was one of those who left the room."

"Yes, good. I'll have to see if we can confirm that, and get a name from someone. Who else?"

"What about Phoebe Wren, sir?" suggested Borthwick. "Could be she was lying about not knowing him."

"Again, yes, quite possible. But what about someone like Morgan – for all we know he has a daughter, or perhaps a niece or something. I'll make some enquiries.

"Tomorrow's job for you, Gemmill, is likely to take a lot longer. Go to Records. Not sure if you can do that here, or if what I want is held in the individual Divisions. On reflection, though, it'll probably be easier to go to the coroners – talk to some coroner's officers. I want to know the name of every woman who died as a result of an illegal abortion between January and April 1938. No, better make it between January and May. We'll have to assume this was in London.

"It's just possible that if we get a surname, we can link that with someone in Douglas House.

"Now, have either of you got any more thoughts?"

"If this was a servant, sir, surely they wouldn't be so accustomed to firearms as most of the upper-class suspects would be? And they might even find it harder to get hold of a pistol?"

"Perhaps. The three footmen are certainly too young to have served in the war – or to have daughters. But Mrs F told me that Morgan left the household in 1914 to serve in the army, and returned later to become butler. He must have used firearms.

"And, sadly it isn't too hard nowadays for

anyone to get hold of an illegal weapon."

"But you need a good lot of cash for that, sir," said Gemmill, "where would a servant get that sort of money? Rumour has it you'd need to pay at least a pony – and for a specialist little gun like the one here, I should think maybe a ton."

"Another good point. And even if money was no object, which crooked gun merchant would have such a pistol? Still, the killer got it somehow."

"All right; let's go home now, and meet up here at half past eight in the morning."

CHAPTER 12

On Thursday morning, the three detectives and Mrs Haskell were all in the DCI's office by eight twenty-five.

"Just a recap of where we are," the DCI began. "If this murder is indeed connected to Hardingham's predilection for sexual relations with women, then there seem to be two main strands.

"First, something could have occurred just before he went abroad, but because he was out of reach, the revenge has only now become possible. That could have involved someone from any class of society. A sort of sub-category there is this abortion business – that probably, but not necessarily, involved someone from the lower classes.

"Second, some incident occurred after he returned. That is where the diary would have been helpful if it had given the full names of his inamoratas – but it is what it is. I wonder if the plural should be inamoratae," he muttered inconsequentially, following that up with "no, I think not."

Adair stopped speaking, and Gemmill took the opportunity to ask a question that he had been pondering since the previous day.

"Yesterday, sir, when you were talking to Lord Hardingham, you said something about who benefits 'financially or otherwise'. What sort of thing did you mean by 'otherwise'?"

"Ah, yes. Well, you were present when Mrs F reported what Hardingham said on being told of his son's death. He as good as said it was for the best. Both Hardingham and his second son could be said to have benefitted. The father benefits by not having to deal with more paternity suits and scandals, and the younger son benefits by now being in line to inherit the title, and probably far more money. Of course, as neither was present in Douglas House there would have had to be an accomplice. That is very, very far-fetched, but nevertheless both must be considered as accessories before the fact.

Adair unlocked the drawer where he had placed the three diaries, and handed the most recent to his Secretary. "Okay, you and Sergeant Borthwick get going with that.

"Gemmill, start with the offices of Mr Bentley Purchase and Mr Oddie. I know Mr Oddie is due to retire – he may even have left already, but this incident would have occurred during his regime. See what you can glean there. Those two gentlemen cover a good chunk of London, but it may be necessary to contact coroners further afield – in Surrey and the City, for example.

"As I said earlier, I very much doubt if this unfortunate woman was from the upper classes, so as well as names I want to know occupations, if any.

"Off you go. Make your calls from your room – I need to use this telephone."

Left to himself, Adair pulled the telephone a little nearer, and picked up the handset. As he did so he leaned back, tilting his chair on to two legs, and putting his feet up on the desk. Conscious that he was getting into bad habits of late, and that one day the chair would topple over, he nevertheless remained in that position.

He gave the Douglas House number to the Yard's switchboard operator and waited, wondering if Mrs Forbes-Kerr and her guests were still at breakfast – or perhaps hadn't even started yet.

"Mrs Forbes-Kerr's residence," the unmistakable orotund voice of the Butler came through the receiver.

Adair identified himself, and asked Morgan to ascertain if it would be convenient to come and talk to the Mistress at ten o'clock.

"She has no appointments to my knowledge, sir," replied the Butler, "but if you wait one moment I will go and enquire."

He was back within two minutes. "That will be perfectly convenient, sir. Madam says that as there are still some guests present, she will see you in the study again."

Adair took his feet off the table, returned his chair to the upright position, and replaced the handset on its rest. With a deep sigh, he reached across to his in-tray, and pulled out a folder. He spent the next thirty minutes reading memoranda and initialling reports, interrupted twice by telephone calls. He was then agreeably surprised when both his sergeants returned together,

"Don't tell me you've finished?'

Both men nodded.

"Mrs H typed the list of names, sir," began Borthwick, "and the two of us cross-checked that with the list you gave us. Not a single Christian name appears on both lists. Sorry."

"Nothing to be sorry about. You look a bit happier, Gemmill – what did you find?"

"I was pleased that there were fewer of these tragedies than I'd feared, sir. I only found two between the dates you specified, both in Mr Purchase's domain.

"One was Agnes Yates, aged twenty-two, and the other was Doris Peters, aged eighteen. Both were domestic servants. I have the addresses of their employers, sir – different houses, but both in Mayfair."

"Well done.

"Borthwick, just look through the most recent diary you were working on. Between say December the year before last and March last year, is there any mention of either Doris or Agnes?"

The DS flipped through the diary, and looked up again within a minute.

"No Doris, sir, but there's an Agnes – well, it says 'Aggie'. And there's a circle around the name, and an exclamation mark. No other names are distinguished like that."

"Good. It proves nothing, of course, but it's very suggestive. And we'll still check on Doris.

"Your next job, then, Gemmill, is to go and call at both houses. Take a car. Don't say you're investigating our case; imply that you are following up on the illegal abortion and the death of the girl. It may be best to try and speak to other servants, either instead of or as well as the householder. Find out everything you can. Play it by ear – it may be possible to find out if Hardingham was a visitor to that house without asking the question directly. Try to get details of the next of kin for each of the dead girls.

"Push as hard as you need to, but just remember that it's possible neither of these sad cases has anything to do with Hardingham.

"When you've done those visits, Gemmill, come and join Borthwick and me at Douglas House. We're going to talk to the staff now.

"Also, when you saw me away with the fairies again yesterday, Gemmill, I was just thinking about the pistol. I have a question for Mrs F before I develop that thought."

***

At Douglas House, Adair and Borthwick were shown into the study by a maid, who said she would inform the mistress that the policemen had arrived. They were not kept waiting for more than two minutes, as Mrs Forbes-Kerr swept into the room and waved the detectives to chairs.

"I've been in something of a quandary, gentlemen," she announced almost before she was seated. "One really should be wearing black, but on the other hand that will cause questions to be asked about who has died. Also, one might not feel quite the same need to show respect in this particular case. So I have abandoned the conventions, and as my guests haven't come with mourning outfits anyway we are carrying on as normal.

"How can I help you today? I assume you have spoken to Lord Hardingham?"

"We have, ma'am, yes. He gave us a lot of very useful background information about his late son. However, we are here today principally to interview your staff. You'll recall that when you first spoke to me you said the murderer must be one of your guests. Initially, I concurred. However, it is just possible that our conclusion was wrong. So I want to speak to every one of your employees, right down to the boot boy. Perhaps we could start with Miss Barnes – we can go to her office if that is more convenient?"

"Oh no, I'll tell her to come here, Chief Inspector. Do you want the others in any particular order?"

"No; whatever is most convenient. I don't anticipate each interview will take above five minutes.

"Just one other question for you, ma'am. Your country house – had Mr Hardingham ever been there?"

"Never. I don't use Morlands much myself, nowadays. I was there for a week at the beginning of this month, but I spend the bulk of my time here now. The house is mostly shut up, and even when I do go down I don't entertain on any scale. Lunch for local county friends, that sort of thing, and no overnight guests. I'd like to sell it – the bulk of the estate was sold soon after my husband died, and just the house and garden remain. But nobody wants houses like mine at present."

"So who looks after the house when you aren't there, ma'am?"

"Oh, there are two housemaids and two gardeners. My old land agent doesn't technically work for me any more, of course, but with the agreement of the new estate owner he keeps an eye on the place and arranges for maintenance work and so on.

"When I stay there, the maids open up a handful of rooms, and two or three of my London staff travel down a day or so in advance. Then more go down the same day as I do.

"You're thinking of this gun, I imagine?"

"If the killer turns out to be a member of your staff, ma'am, it would seem possible that the pistol could have come from Morlands.

"Which of your staff were there on your most recent visit?"

"All of them except Bernice and young Higgins. Oh, and the scullery maids don't go either.

"Eileen came with me once, a couple of years ago, but since then she has always remained here, to deal with letters, telephone calls, and so on. I speak to her on the telephone almost every day when I'm at Morlands."

Mrs Forbes-Kerr thought for a minute.

"Frederick did have a number of firearms of various sorts, and he may well have acquired more in the years when I didn't visit the gun room. All I can say is that I never heard him mention anything with a silencer."

"It now seems the shot was muffled with a heavy towel, ma'am, so it is probable that there wasn't a silencer after all."

"I see. Will you want to go and look in the gun room, Chief Inspector? I am ashamed to admit it, but I don't even know if Frederick even kept a list of what he owned. If he did have an inventory, it might be in his study, which has also hardly been entered since his death."

"Yes, I'd like to send someone down there later today or tomorrow. Where is the house?"

"It's in Burford Parva. Take the A31 towards Winchester, and turn off to the left about twelve miles past Aldershot. The turning is signposted to Burford Magna, but you reach Morlands before you get there. The smaller parish contains very few residences other than Morlands.

"I'll telephone Rhoda, the senior maid, and tell her to expect someone."

"Thank you ma'am – but please don't mention the gun room on the telephone."

"I understand; if that's all I'll send Eileen in to see you. Just ring if you want refreshments."

***

When Mrs Forbes-Kerr had gone, Borthwick smiled at his boss.

"You think one of the servants took the pistol during the last visit, sir?"

"Well, it depends first of all on whether the late Frederick owned a Liliput. It also depends on whether the murderer was a servant rather than one of the guests as I originally assumed.

"But given that Mrs F had apparently told at least one person – before the date of that trip to Hampshire – that Mr Hardingham was to be a guest, it seems a possibility. Miss Barnes definitely knew he was coming, and it may be that she mentioned the names to others, or that Mrs F did so. Certainly the Cook would have had to be advised of numbers in advance, so perhaps the names were given to her.

"Anyway, when Gemmill arrives, I'm going to send him down into the rural depths of Hampshire."

"Do you think there could have been a conspiracy between one of the servants and one of the guests, sir?"

"Extremely unlikely, although not impossible. If it was one of the guests after all, it seems more probable that the pistol came from some other source, and so the guest would have no need to risk engaging in a conspiracy."

There was a knock on the door, and a woman entered the room. Everything about her could be described as 'ordinary'. She was a little over forty, about five feet two inches tall, with mouse-coloured hair done in a bun, and was dressed in a very plain unpatterned navy-blue summer dress. No jewellery was visible on hands, ears, wrists, or dress. A pair of spectacles hung on a cord from her neck.

Her face would never be one to turn men's heads, but it did suggest the owner possessed intelligence. The eyes gleamed as she shook Adair's outstretched hand.

"This is Sergeant Borthwick, Miss Barnes. Please take a seat.

"We won't keep you long. Had you met the late Mr Hardingham before?"

"I hadn't even heard of him until Mrs Forbes-Kerr said she wanted to invite him here. I'd met his father, of course – he and Lady Hardingham have been dinner guests here several times – but I knew nothing of his offspring."

"So when you were asked to arrange this particular visit, how did you contact him?"

"I had Lord Hardingham's telephone number, so I called that. I think it was the Butler that I spoke to, and when I said that I needed to contact Jocelyn Hardingham, the man informed me that he had his own residence. I was given the address, and I wrote to Jocelyn indicating Mrs Forbes-Kerr's wishes, and asking if he could provide a number of convenient dates.

"You see, it was made clear that I was to ensure that he was to be present – together with Lady Phoebe Wren. The others could just attend if convenient. I contacted her at the same time. Both telephoned me soon after receiving their letters, saying they appreciated Mrs Forbes-Kerr's provisional invitation. Lady Phoebe offered several dates, but Jocelyn said he could come on any day.

"So I chose a date, and prepared formal invitations for them and the others on the list, for Mrs Forbes-Kerr to sign. We had anticipated that three of four of the invitees would be unable to come, but in fact everyone accepted, which was a bit of a strain as far as the overnight guests were concerned."

"Did you tell Jocelyn that there was some attempted matchmaking going on?"

"Not initially. When I spoke to him on the telephone, the invitation was only for dinner. It was when I was preparing the formal invitations that I was told to add the suggestion that certain guests should stay overnight. When Jocelyn received his, he called me again, obviously surprised. I did mention then that he was to meet what had been described to me as 'a suitable young lady'. I did tell him her name, and he said something like 'good; I wanted to meet her anyway'."

"On what date, roughly, were the invitations confirmed?"

"I'd have to check in my records, but I should think around the twenty-fifth of July."

"And on what date did most of the household decamp to Morlands?"

"On the first of August. They were away for seven nights."

"One last thing, Miss Barnes. Who in this house, apart from Mrs Forbes-Kerr and yourself, knew the names on that guest list before they travelled down to Hampshire?"

The Social Secretary considered the question.

"I can't be certain who actually knew, but the answer is that any of the servants might have known. You see, every time we have a function here – whether that's afternoon tea for two of Madam's friends, or a big formal or semi-formal dinner, it's my job to mark that not only in her diary, but also on a calendar in the kitchen. And beside the calendar is a sheaf of papers clipped to a notice board, in date order. Each paper shows the guests coming to a particular function. It also shows, for example, if a particular guest doesn't eat pork, or even any meat.

"We don't have a housekeeper, but Morgan and Dorcas Warren carry out that role between them. They need the list to see how many bedrooms will be needed and who to allocate to each; how many places are to be set for dinner, and how much food to order – those sorts of things.

"I would have posted the list of guests within a day of getting the last acceptance – so almost certainly four or five days before the move to Morlands. Any of the staff could have read it."

"Sorry – a supplementary. When you were making the arrangements, and perhaps speaking to other invitees, did you inform any of them about who else was on the guest list?"

"Definitely not. You see, it is very well known that invitations to this house are, shall we say, only issued to an exclusive few. It would never be necessary to drop other names to anyone in order to persuade him or her to attend. I only mentioned Lady Phoebe – and probably should not have done – because Jocelyn seemed to be hesitant."

The DCI thanked Miss Barnes, and she left the room.

"Your theory looks to be feasible, sir," remarked Borthwick.

"Still feels like clutching at straws, though.

Press the bell, please."

CHAPTER 13

Within a minute, the Butler arrived.

"You rang, sir?"

"Yes, Morgan. Having interviewed the guests yesterday, it the turn of the staff today. Each will only be tied up for five or ten minutes. Is it convenient for you to go first?"

"Oh yes, sir – glad to get it out of the way!"

"Good; do take a seat then.

"Now, had you come across Mr Hardingham before his visit?"

"No, sir. His father had been here before, but the son never."

"When did you first learn that Mr Hardingham was to be coming to the house?"

"I can't give the exact date, sir, but it must have been about a month ago. Miss Barnes notifies Mrs Warren and me that visitors will be attending something that has been arranged – sometimes it's just a meal, and sometimes it involves guests staying overnight. As this one did. She marks the date on the kitchen calendar, and gives us a list of those who have been invited."

"Yes, that confirms what she told us. Who else looks at that list?"

"Well, only Mrs Warren needs to, sir. But I imagine every one of the servants looks at it – everyone is interested in which important people are coming. And the footmen and maids who will be waiting at table, or taking early morning tea to the bedrooms, will be keen to know who they'll be encountering."

"I can understand that. The visitors to this household must often be very famous people."

"You can say that again, sir. Although the present King hasn't yet graced us with his presence, his three brothers – the Dukes of Windsor, Gloucester and Kent – have all been here, and his late father, George the Fifth, came while the Master was alive. In my time in the household, every prime minister has accepted an invitation – including, perhaps surprisingly, Mr Ramsay MacDonald."

"Impressive indeed. Now, the country house, Morlands. You and most of the staff spent a week there at the beginning of this month, I understand?"

"That is so, sir. Most of us accompany the Mistress, as she no longer has a full complement of staff down there."

"She told us that most of the rooms are shut up, now, and also that she hasn't been in some – the gun room for example – since her husband died."

"I can well believe that, sir. I heard that the Mistress did some coarse shooting when she was a lot younger, but I've never seen her take a gun out since I joined the household as a footman back in 1913.

"What about the study?"

"Ah, well, that was the Master's sort of retreat, as you might say. It was actually in that room where he collapsed and died. So the Mistress never uses it now."

"Do you go in the gun room yourself when you're down at Morlands?"

"I have never set foot in it, sir. When the Master was alive, he employed two footmen who had been taught how to clean shotguns. And my remit did not include supervising that work.

Since the Master died, there has never been a shooting party, so the room isn't used. I've never heard the Mistress discuss the matter, but I imagine the room is just as it was the day he left us.

"But you wouldn't be asking these questions if you didn't think the gun that killed Mr Hardingham came from Morlands. Well, I suppose it's possible. The Master did have some side arms – he used to bring one out sometimes and shoot at a target on the lawn.

"But I assure you that I didn't bring back a pistol from Morlands, sir, and nor did I shoot the man."

"A change of subject, then," said Adair, now looking very closely at Morgan. "Do the names

Agnes Yates or Doris Peters mean anything to you?"

"Neither name rings a bell, sir. Are they servants, or of the quality?"

"Servants, I think."

"Well, neither has been employed in this house in the twenty-five years I've been here. May I ask what is the connection with Mr Hardingham's death?"

"I can't say. There may be none. But they're both dead too.

"Do you have any children yourself?"

"Alas no, sir, I married at the end of the Great War – to a housemaid in the service of The Duke of Wellington a few doors along, as a matter of fact. Within four months, my wife died in the influenza epidemic. His Grace was very good about it – he paid for a nice funeral and so on – and after the service he talked to me about joining his staff – he said his own butler would be retiring within a couple of years and I would stand a good chance of getting the post. I was happy here though, and a matter of days later our butler died in the same epidemic, and the Master promoted me."

"All right, Morgan, thank you. Please ask someone else to come and see us – and do not mention those two names to anyone at all – you understand?"

"Perfectly; you can rely on my discretion. I'll send in the first person I see. Also some coffee, sir."

After the Butler left, neither Adair nor

Borthwick spoke. The Sergeant appeared to be going over his notes, and the DCI, although not in one of his trances, was staring out of the window in thought.

Two minutes passed, and then a footman tapped on the door and came in.

"I'm Patrick Rafferty, sir," the man announced; "I think you want to talk to me?"

The detectives hadn't seen this footman before. Like all the staff, he was smartly dressed. Whereas the Butler wore a black tail coat, Rafferty was in the yellow and black uniform typical of someone doing his job.

"Sit down, Patrick. I assume you are addressed by your Christian name here? We policemen don't often use those when talking to suspects, but we'll stick to the conventions of the house."

Adair put the same questions to Patrick as he had to Morgan. The footman said he had never heard of Hardingham before. He admitted that he had seen the guest list before travelling to Hampshire. He had never been in the gun room. He showed no flicker of emotion when asked about the two girls, and denied ever knowing anyone with these names.

After only seven or eight minutes Adair sent him on his way, and as he left the room a maid came in carrying a tray.

"Some refreshments for you, gentlemen, and Mr Morgan says I must stay so you can question me. I'm Estelle Bates."

"Thank you, Estelle; most welcome. Sit down, please."

Both officers took a cup and added cream but not sugar. Each took a biscuit, and then looked at Estelle. They saw a girl in her mid-twenties, a little overweight but not unattractive. Her cap was perched on top of her head, and not for the first time Adair wondered what was the point of the cap at all.

He went through the routine questions, and heard nothing new. Estelle mentioned that she had been in the dining room when Doctor Knowles had informed the Mistress about the murder.

"Quite a shock it was to me, sir, and the guests were surprised too – but they all sort of brushed it aside pretty soon. What they call the stiff upper lip, I suppose."

Over the next ninety minutes, all the remaining servants passed through the interview process. Most said they had looked at the guest list well before the day of the dinner. None had ever heard of Jocelyn Hardingham before. None showed any emotion at the mention of the two dead girls.

The only one with anything different to say was the unfortunate Niamh, who recounted with a curious combination of horror and glee how she had discovered the body.

"Just staring at the ceiling, he was. 'Course, 'til I drew the curtains I didn't see that. Touched his head, and he was cold. Fair made me sick, it did."

Higgins was the last to be seen. He had apparently never left the lower ground floor since joining the household, and was visibly awed by the ambiance of the study. Curious, the DCI asked him how he received the boots and shoes he was to clean, and learned that Bernice or another maid brought them down to him, and returned them to their owners' rooms later. The word 'troglodyte' came to Adair's mind, but the boy seemed remarkably cheerful.

Higgins' departure coincided with the arrival of Morgan, escorting Sergeant Gemmill.

"I imagine you are ready for some lunch, gentlemen," said the Butler. "I will have some food sent up shortly."

As soon as the door closed behind Morgan, Gemmill started to speak.

"One failure, sir, but I think the other is good. No success with Doris Peters. It seems she was an orphan, brought up in a Barnardo's home. She had no boyfriends, so far as anyone knew.

"But Agnes Yates is hopeful. She worked for a Mr Walter Farncombe, in Upper Brook Street. It is a very small household, sir, although it's quite a big house. – a valet and there used to be two maids. It seems Agnes was never replaced, though. Mr Farncombe is a bachelor.

"When I called, both the master and the valet were out, but I talked to the remaining maid

– Sylvia Drake. It upset her to speak about Agnes – they were friends as well as colleagues. But she said three things which seem important.

"First, Farncombe, who sounds about the same age as Hardingham, often holds what Sylvia calls parties. Usually three or four young men, and invariably a few young women. She doesn't know names – the visitors are never introduced to the staff. Sylvia doesn't like these parties – she was very reluctant to talk about them – and she would like to find another post. But she did say Farncombe pays very well.

"Second, she says Agnes was 'walking out' with a young man – not one of these upper-class men, but someone who worked in a big house. Sylvia saw him two or three times, and talked to him on one occasion. She says he wasn't a Londoner, but had a sort of burr in his voice. She admits she's not good at regional accents, but she thought he might come from down southwest somewhere.

"His name was Sam.

"Third, she said she didn't know Agnes had been pregnant until after she died. Apparently she'd had an afternoon off a couple of days before she died, and came back very upset, and soon after became ill – Sylvia said she seemed to have a lot of pain in her tummy, but she refused to have help. She could hardly work the next day or so, and the next night an ambulance was called. Agnes died on the way to hospital, although the household didn't know that until lunchtime the next day, when a detective arrived.

"Sylvia opened the door to him, and he said he'd come about Agnes's death – that's when she heard not only about the death but that the autopsy had shown it was probably the result of a botched abortion. He said he would need to question everyone in the house.

"So Sylvia asked his name – it was Hastings – and showed him in to see Farncombe. And that was the last she saw of Hastings.

"She believes that her master must have bribed the police officer to drop the criminal enquiry. And she says, very convincingly I think, that if that happened it would mean that the father was likely to be either Farncombe or one of his rich cronies.

"The inquest returned an open verdict, and it was fortunate that when I was making enquiries in the coroners' offices the clerk I spoke to included this case.

"I warned Sylvia not to mention to her master or the valet that I'd called – I got the impression she wouldn't have done so anyway."

"Well done, Sergeant. Excellent, in fact. We'll come back to the alleged bribery in a minute, but let's look at the boyfriend first. Could be a coincidence, of course, but in this 'big house' we have a servant named Samuel Owen – who also happens to have a Dorset or perhaps Hampshire accent."

"He didn't show any reaction when the name Agnes Yates was put to him though," observed Borthwick.

"No, he didn't. Mind you, I imagine that whatever I'd said about not telling anyone else about those two names, I bet the earlier interviewees blabbed them – and the later ones could then be prepared.

"What other difficulties do we have, gentlemen?"

"The pistol, sir?" suggested Gemmill.

"Yes; and when we've had something to eat you are going down to the country house in Hampshire. The skeleton staff there are expecting you. Look in the gun room, and in the late master's study. I want evidence – a list, a purchase invoice, anything – to confirm that there was such a pistol in that house. That'll be a start.

"What else?"

There was silence for a few seconds.

"It'll be very hard to prove that Owen – if it's him – knew who the father of the baby was," said Borthwick, "We can't ask Agnes if she told him."

"That's right," replied Adair. "So we come back to the police investigation. It is certainly very odd that Sylvia was never questioned by this Hastings man – especially after he said he would be doing so. I'll talk to the DDI at Vine Street.

"You said the abortionist was never identified – and I wonder if Owen was even aware that she was going to visit one."

The DCI was about to say something else, when the Butler arrived, leading two maids, each pushing a trolley.

Gemmill, who hadn't seen the previous day's repast, watched in disbelief as the food was laid out, and Morgan deftly uncorked a bottle of wine, again offering a sample for the DCI to approve.

"Is it three teas, gentlemen?" queried the Butler. All three detectives nodded.

"Very well; in about fifteen minutes, then."

Morgan shepherded the maids out, and Gemmill burst out laughing.

"Blimey, sir, how the other half live! I wish all our cases involved this sort of attention."

Adair grinned.

"Indeed. Yesterday the trifle was excellent, but neither of us could manage a portion until later in the afternoon. Today I see we have what looks like gooseberry fool. I'm salivating already!"

Half an hour later, Adair announced that it was time to get back to work.

"You get off to Hampshire, Gemmill. By the time you've been there and back, it'll be late, so go straight home and we'll see you tomorrow morning.

"You and I will go back to the Yard, Borthwick. I'm going to try to speak to the C Division DDI. Then we may go and talk to Farncombe – and the maid and the valet."

"Aren't you going to interview Owen again, sir?" asked Borthwick in surprise.

"Too soon; we don't have enough yet. We may never get any more, of course."

CHAPTER 14

Back at Scotland Yard, Adair said he would make some calls, and told Borthwick to get on with something from another case.

Upstairs, his Secretary handed him three slips of paper with messages, and the DCI took these into his own office, closed the door, and sat down at his desk.

The first message said that the Assistant Commissioner would like a brief oral report on the Douglas House case first thing next morning. The other messages had no connection with the current case, and two quick telephone calls disposed of those matters.

Adair pick up the telephone again, and asked for Vine Street. On being connected, he identified himself to the station switchboard operator, and asked to be put through to the Divisional Detective Inspector. This officer, an old acquaintance, was at his desk.

"Good afternoon, Will – David Adair here. I assume your Super has told you that the Douglas House murder has been given to the Yard?"

"Oh yes, sir – and I'm very pleased about it! I've got far too much on my plate as it is. Just hearing the address made me think rather you than me. Are you after manpower? I really can't spare anyone from CID, but we might find a couple of uniformed men."

"No, it's not that. Do you recall the death of a young servant girl a few months ago – back street abortion job?"

"I remember the incident, sir, yes. Is that connected with your murder?"

"Very possibly. I'm lacking evidence as yet, but it may just be that the victim was the father of the baby that was being aborted. If that is the case, it would provide a motive. But your man Hastings – I assume he's a DC – seems to have given up the investigation very quickly. Nobody seems to have been interviewed in the household where the girl worked, and the abortionist was never found. What do you know?"

"I only remember that Hastings – he is a DC – said nobody even knew the girl was pregnant. He put forward a hypothesis that she was moonlighting as a prostitute for some extra money, and fell pregnant that way. He said it was pointless wasting any more time on the case. I recall that he pointed out that although the PM confirmed there had been a recent abortion, and that was very likely the cause of death, the pathologist couldn't say that was definitely the case. As a result I think the Coroner had to bring in an open verdict"

"What's Hastings like, Will?"

The DDI hesitated. "Let's just say he's well into his forties, and will never progress any higher."

"Might he accept a bribe?" asked Adair bluntly.

Once again the DDI hesitated. "I heard a rumour once, about fifteen months ago. I had Hastings on the carpet, but there was no evidence whatsoever, and I had to let it go."

"OK, Will. Is he around this afternoon? If he's available, I'd appreciate it if you would send him along to the Yard. I'll not keep him more than quarter of an hour."

"I'll see if he is in. If he is, I'll get him to you within half an hour. If he isn't, I'll call you back to inform you, and we can perhaps fix an appointment for tomorrow."

The DDI called back twenty minutes later.

"Hastings is on the way to you, sir – should arrive within ten minutes. I've been to our records room to dig out the file. You said nobody in the household was interviewed. That's not what Hastings says. His report says that he spoke to the householder, a Walter Farncombe, the valet, Clement Ellison, and a maid, Sylvia Drake. They all said they were not aware of the girl's pregnancy, and had no idea who the father might be.

"Is that any use to you?"

"Yes, indeed; thanks. I'm only concerned

with my murder – if there are any other shenanigans, I'll leave those to you."

After ending the call, Adair rang down to the CID general office, and asked Borthwick to come upstairs.

"I have a C Division DC coming in, Sergeant, and I want you to take notes and bear witness. He's the one Gemmill told us about earlier. Sit here beside me."

Before Borthwick could speak, Adair's Secretary tapped at the door and announced, "Constable Hastings to see you, sir."

Come in and sit down," instructed the DCI. "Did Mr Watkinson tell you why I wanted to see you?"

"No sir," replied Hastings; a very thin man of average height, aged, as the DDI had said, in his mid-forties. A detective ideally has no features to make people turn and look at him, and Hastings certainly fulfilled that requirement.

"I'm interested in the young woman, Agnes Yates, who died as a result of a botched abortion. Tell me about that case."

Both Adair and Borthwick thought that Hastings' face suddenly changed, with an instant expression of surprise followed immediately by one of caution or reserve.

"It wasn't proved that she died from the abortion, sir. The pathologist said it appeared that way but he couldn't rule out some other cause."

"You're splitting hairs, Hastings. The fact is

that she had undergone an illegal abortion, a day or two before she died. What enquiries did you make?"

Hastings hesitated.

"The girl was a servant in Mr Farncombe's house just off Park Lane, sir. There was also a valet and another parlourmaid. They knew nothing of the pregnancy, nor of who might have been the father of the child. No leads, so I couldn't even start to track down the abortionist."

"All three of them told you they knew nothing?"

"That's correct, sir."

Adair stared at the Constable for half a minute, without speaking. Hastings began to twitch.

"How much did Farncombe pay you, Hastings?" the DCI shot the question out bluntly.

The Constable half rose from his chair, and spluttered "I don't know what you mean!"

"Sit down," barked Adair. "The only time Miss Drake spoke to you was when she took you in to see Farncombe. You told her you would be coming back to interview her, but you never did. She could have told you, for example, who the dead girl's boyfriend had been – and clearly you should have interviewed him as well, as it was likely that he knew who had performed the abortion.

"You lied in your case report, and you've lied again this afternoon. I repeat my question, and the sooner you answer it truthfully the better – how much were you paid to hush all this up?"

Hastings visibly squirmed around on his chair, and avoided eye contact with either officer facing him.

Eventually, looking down at the desk in front of him, he replied in a low voice, "seventy-five pounds."

"I see. Did Farncombe tell you who was the father – him or one of his friends, for example?"

"No sir, honest. He just suggested that I put it out that nobody in the house knew anything about it, and he suggested I say that the girl was believed to be a part-time prostitute who must have slipped up."

"You don't know what 'honest' means, Hastings, but I do believe that is what he said."

The DCI pushed a pad of paper and a fountain pen across the desk. "Write a statement now, saying what you've just told us. You know how to start it off. Just a few sentences will do ."

Hastings obediently began to write, while the other two sat watching. It only took three minutes, and he pushed the pad back to Adair.

"That'll do. Sign it.

"Right," he continued when that was done, "let me tell you why I'm interested in your matter.

"The dead girl's boyfriend is a key suspect in the murder of an upper-class man who was a notorious womaniser. It may well be that the murder victim is the father of the aborted baby – there doesn't seem to be any other possible motive.

Now, given Farncombe is keen to hush everything up, it seems likely that he knows or at least suspects that a friend of his was involved.

"Anyway, you'll almost certainly be charged with malfeasance in public office, and probably with conspiracy – together with Farncombe – to pervert the course of justice.

"I'm not going to arrest you – I'll leave that to your superiors in Vine Street. But I am going to suspend you from duty, unless you choose to write out your resignation here and now."

Hastings appeared to be in shock, but he took the pad again and scribbled out a few words, and signed underneath.

"Hand over your badge and warrant card," ordered Adair.

"All right, take him downstairs, Sergeant, and see him safely off the premises."

Borthwick returned a few minutes later.

"Blimey, sir, what an idiot. I've not come across malfeasance or whatever you said. What's that?"

"It's a Common Law offence dating back about seven hundred years. It is committed if a holder of a public office acts – or fails to act – in an appropriate manner according to the duties of his office. It carries a sentence of up to life imprisonment. As does conspiracy.

"Whether Hastings is charged is doubtful, actually. The Met doesn't like washing its dirty linen in public.

"Anyway, I must let his DDI know what's transpired, and then we'll go and see Farncombe. If he isn't in, we'll start off with his staff. Get the car, and I'll meet you in the car park in a few minutes."

It took only a few minutes to explain to Inspector Watkinson what had happened. The DDI was not surprised.

"I guessed that would be the outcome, as soon as you asked to see him," he remarked. "He won't be missed.

"I'll have to take advice on how to deal with this, sir – but of course if you charge Farncombe with conspiracy then Hastings will have to be charged with that too."

"Yes, but I am only really interested in the murder case – I might just threaten Farncombe in order to get confirmation that the father of the aborted baby was one of his guests. I'll keep you informed."

Adair put down the telephone, and stood up to go. He had just reached the door when the telephone rang again.

For a moment the DCI was minded to ignore it and carry on, but then decided to turn back, muttering to himself. He picked up the instrument again.

"Adair here...Yes...Oh, yes m'lady...I see."

He listened in silence for some thirty seconds.

"Very helpful indeed, m'lady, that confirms something we have heard from another source. I assume your daughters never went to this place themselves...Just hearsay...I see, yes... I'm very pleased to know that. Please convey my thanks to your daughters...Yes, I'll do that. Thanks again, goodbye."

CHAPTER 15

The period of loan for the Railton had expired, so the detectives were in a standard unmarked Wolseley. On the short journey, Adair passed on to the Sergeant the information which Lady Wymondham had just given him.

Borthwick was able to park within a few yards of their destination. He rang the bell, and the door was opened by a man who was clearly the valet.

Adair identified himself and his colleague, and asked to see Mr Farncombe.

"He is at home, sir – if you care to step inside, I'll see if he is available to see you."

The DCI said nothing, and the two were shown into what the man said was the morning room. Neither sat down.

"What will you say if he isn't 'available', sir?"

"I'm confident that he will be, Sergeant. It's just a conventional remark – although it seems the maid didn't follow that convention when Hastings called."

Two minutes later, the door opened, and a

man in his shirtsleeves walked into the room. He was of average height, in his early thirties, with a good head of very fair hair.

"Police? How can I help? Do sit down. Scotland Yard? Extraordinary." Farncombe spoke these sentences without any pause in between each.

"We're investigating the murder of Jocelyn Hardingham. Did you know him, sir?"

"Slightly, yes. And I read about his murder in the newspaper. Shocking. But I certainly didn't kill him, so I don't see how I can help you."

"Oh, there's no suggestion that you killed him, sir. We have other suspects. But I want to go back a year or so. You had a maid here then – Agnes Yates. Yes?"

Farncombe seemed to hesitate for a moment, but then confirmed what the DCI had said.

"She died in rather tragic circumstances, did she not?"

"Yes. It seemed that she had fallen pregnant, and had an abortion, although I believe it was never proved that her death was a direct result of that."

"Were you not interested in how she came to be pregnant – and weren't you concerned to assist in helping the police to trace the abortionist?"

"How could I help? I didn't know the wretched girl was even pregnant, and I had no information about whoever carried out the abortion."

"Really. If you knew nothing about how she came to be pregnant, why did you find it necessary to bribe the police officer who came to make enquiries?"

"What a scandalous suggestion, Chief Inspector," shouted Farncombe, jumping up from his chair. "I'll have you pounding a beat for this. Get out of my house at once."

Adair didn't move.

"Sit down, Farncombe. When we leave this house it'll likely be with you coming with us – in handcuffs."

Farncombe glowered at the DCI, but slumped back into his chair.

"Constable Hastings has already made a full confession, so there's no point in your denying the facts.

"It's really only a question of what to charge you with. Bribery of a police officer is a misdemeanour, carrying a sentence of two years' imprisonment.

"Or we could go for conspiracy to pervert the course of justice – that might be better, as it carries up to life imprisonment.

"So let's stop playing games. You don't risk trying to bribe a police officer unless you have a very, very good reason for doing so. In this case, it was because you knew something which you didn't want made public. Suppose you tell us what that was."

"I just didn't want the scandal of this girl's death attached to me or my household, I suppose."

"Won't do, Farncombe. You knew a lot more about this sorry affair than you suggested a few minutes ago.

"I'm sure you knew, for example, that the girl had been raped – by one of your friends. It was that you were trying to cover up. And the scandal would indeed have attached itself to you, because the incident happened during one of your so-called 'parties. 'Orgies' might be a more appropriate word.

"Talk. I must warn you that although you are not obliged to say anything, whatever you do say will be taken down and may be used in evidence at your trial."

Farncombe was now squirming in his chair. He was looking everywhere but at his inquisitor. A full minute went by, as he was obviously deciding what to do. Eventually, still without looking at the DCI, he spoke.

"All right, yes. Jocelyn did have the girl. I didn't know about it there and then, but a bit later that night she came to me in tears and reported what had happened. Rather than let her go to the police, I basically bought her silence.

"But then, a few weeks later, she said she thought she was pregnant. I thought she might go to the police after all. And although she didn't actually ask for more money I thought that would be the next step.

"So I called Jocelyn, and put him in the picture. He said he would sort it all out. He came here the next day and talked to Aggie. I wasn't present during that conversation, but before he left he said it was all going to be taken care of.

"The next thing I knew was that a few days later Aggie became ill, and quickly died. When the police officer came making enquiries, my first thought was to protect Jocelyn – and retain my good name. I was stupid."

"You certainly were. Inevitably, the information about the assault leaked out – in two ways, it seems. First, your Agnes had a boyfriend, in whom she certainly confided before her death. And second, probably through other friends of yours present that night, it began to be talked about in the upper reaches of society.

"And, as a result, Hardingham has been murdered.

"I'm arresting you on suspicion of conspiring with the late Jocelyn Hardingham to prevent the course of justice. You can have a solicitor, if you want one, when we get you to the police station.

Adair stood up, and looked around for the bellpush. Spotting it, he pressed it hard.

"Stay in this room, Farncombe, and don't think of running away. You and I will have a quick word with the staff, Sergeant."

This time the maid came in response to the ring.

"Good afternoon, Miss. You'll be Sylvia Drake, I expect. We are police officers. I'd like to talk to you, and separately to your colleague Mr Ellison.

"Mr Farncombe is under arrest, and will be staying in this room for the moment. Where can we go to talk?"

The maid hesitated, and then led the detectives to the dining room. Adair indicated that she should sit down.

"All right, Sylvia. I heard from the detective who saw you this morning. The policeman you took through to your master on the earlier occasion is also under arrest. All this must have been very distressing for you, and I'm afraid your job here will be gone – Mr Farncombe is unlikely to be coming back for a long time. I'll give you my card. Give the agency or a prospective employer my details and I'll explain to them why you can't provide the usual reference."

"That's kind of you, sir; don't know what I'd do otherwise."

"Now, I'll need a formal statement from you sometime," continued Adair, "but we can sort that in the next day or so. Please ask Mr Ellison to come and see us now. Don't tell him anything yet."

Two minutes passed, which the DCI spent in admiring the ornate silver centrepiece on the dining table, and Borthwick in looking at a marginally erotic painting on one wall. Farncombe was evidently well-off, but being so young presumably hadn't made the money himself. Adair wondered if he even had a job.

The valet tapped on the door and came in.

"You wished to see me, sir?"

"Yes. You are Clement Ellison, is that correct?"

"It is."

"Sit down. Tell us what you know about the circumstances of Agnes Yates' death – including how and when she fell pregnant. Before you answer, I should tell you that your master is under arrest for conspiring to pervert the course of justice, and the police officer who came immediately after Aggie's death is also under arrest for accepting a bribe when asked to cover things up."

Ellison turned pale, and started to shake.

"I had nothing to do with it, sir," he pleaded.

"The master has these parties, as he calls them. Two or three of his friends, and some ladies – sometimes of the quality but usually high-class prostitutes. Not mixed together, of course.

"Well, one night – over a year ago now – something happened. We had two maids then, and they helped serve food and drinks and so on, but they weren't expected to sort of take part, as it were. Anyway, on this occasion it seemed Aggie got raped. She came down to the servants' hall crying. She talked about going to the police. I gave her a good dose of brandy, and went to find the master.

"He came downstairs, and although I wasn't present I gather he gave her money to stop her reporting the matter.

"Then, a month or two later, she started to be sick in the mornings, and said she must be pregnant. So she spoke to the master again. I honestly don't know what he said, but the Honourable Jocelyn Hardingham came round and spoke to her the next day.

"A day or so after that she fell ill and died."

"I see," said Adair. "Was Mr Hardingham a regular visitor here?"

"Oh yes, sir. At least once a month for several years. But he stopped coming after that incident, and when he came last week it was the first time I'd seen him since."

"Did you actually witness the rape of Aggie Yates?"

"No, sir. There are several bedrooms available to guests."

"Did you procure the abortion for Aggie?"

"Certainly not, sir, and you can't prove that I did."

"What about procuring the call girls for these parties?"

Ellison hesitated.

"I don't want to answer that question," he replied.

"I see. You acted as their pimp, I suppose. I expect we'll be able to find a few of them, and learn that you got a fee. If I can be bothered to pursue this, you'll likely face a charge of living off immoral earnings. I guess we could throw in an extra charge for Farncombe too – keeping a disorderly house, in other words a brothel."

Ellison made no reply, but his face colour was now nearer to green.

"You know Hardingham is dead, I suppose?"

"What? No. But he's no age. Suicide?"

"No, Ellison, he was murdered. Almost certainly in connection with the Aggie business. And it's the murder that I'm principally concerned with, not your sordid activities here.

"So I'm not arresting you now, but I'll be speaking to the Divisional Detective Inspector. I think you did organise the abortion, so my advice to you is to cough up the name of the abortionist very quickly – the DDI might well prefer to have her or him banged up, rather than a miserable specimen of humanity like you.

"Get out now."

Borthwick, who had worked with the DCI for some eighteen months, thought he had never seen his boss treat a criminal so contemptuously before. But he mentally cheered.

"Right, let's collect Farncombe and get him to Vine Street. I'll talk to Mr Watkinson, and he can take over Farncombe and decide what he wants to do about Ellison."

At the police station, Farncombe was handed over to the Custody Sergeant.

"I'm not interviewing you any further,

Farncombe. I'm formally charging you with bribery of a police constable, contrary to Section 2 of the Public Bodies Corrupt Practices Act. I also charge you with conspiring together with Jocelyn Hardingham to pervert the course of justice, contrary to Common Law.

"Book him in for those, Sergeant. Is the DDI still here?

"Yes sir – oh, here he is."

DI Watkinson was evidently on his way home. He smiled a greeting to the Yard officers.

"Got someone for us, I see, sir."

Farncombe was led away, belatedly asking to see a solicitor.

Adair gave the DDI a succinct report.

"I think the charge of conspiracy with the deceased man might not stick, and I think it better not to involve Hastings in an alternative conspiracy charge, although that's up to you. So I've charged Farncombe with bribery as a back-up. I don't think you'll have much of a job in persuading the beak to remand him in custody tomorrow – I still need a statement from the maid and I don't want him throwing her out."

"But the valet should really be pressed to reveal what he knows of the abortionist. Again, I leave that to you.

"I just want one more bit of circumstantial evidence, and then I'll see our murder suspect again. I hope to have another person for your cells tomorrow!"

***

On the way back to the yard, Borthwick remarked on how his boss had seemed to be especially contemptuous of both Farncombe and Ellison.

"Yes, I am, Sergeant. These up-market call girls make a choice to sell their bodies, and as long as they don't solicit in the street and only work in their own house or in the private house of a client, they aren't breaking the law.

"But here an innocent girl has been defiled, and effectively killed. And rich people are colluding in covering it all up.

"As you know, my Sophia is only seven; I'd like to think there are fewer animals like Farncombe and Ellison about when she grows up."

"Hardingham is no loss either, sir."

"Absolutely right. However, we can't have people going around executing people willy-nilly, however obnoxious the victim might be.

"I'll see you in the morning. I have to report to the AC first thing, but I'll call you and Gemmill up when I've seen him.

"Good evening."

CHAPTER 16

At nine o'clock, Adair telephoned the Assistant Commissioner's office, and explained to a secretary that he had been asked to report.

"Oh yes, Chief Inspector, he mentioned it last night. You can come straight up."

Two minutes later, Adair was seated in front of the senior officer, and gave his oral report.

"Excellent," said the AC. "So there was no attempt at obstruction from Douglas House?"

"None at all, sir. On the contrary, Mrs Forbes-Kerr and all her guests were very co-operative. It's Farncombe – and the murder victim himself – who were obstructing justice."

"Yes indeed. I also think it is the right decision not to charge this man from C Division. Dirty washing, and so on. Loss of job and pension will have to do. But if it comes out, well it can't be helped.

"All right, Adair, carry on. Good luck with the rest of the case."

Smiling to himself, as he returned to his own office, the DCI thought he certainly would need some luck to finish the murder case successfully. As he passed his Secretary's room, he asked her to find Sergeants Gemmill and Borthwick, and tell them to come up at once.

"'Morning sir," chorused the two men as they came into the room a few minutes later.

"And a very good morning to you two," replied Adair with a smile. "No doubt each of you has told the other about yesterday. So now you can tell me what you found at Morlands, Gemmill. Go on – ruin my day by telling me there was nothing."

"Oh no, sir, as good as we could have hoped for. I was greeted at the door by both of the two maids – the skeleton staff, they call themselves, which is not exactly apt as I should think both weigh well over sixteen stone. They don't see many people nowadays, it seems. So they both escorted me to the late master's study. Apart from dusting it every so often, the room hasn't been touched since his death, they told me.

"Anyway, in a desk drawer I found what seemed to be a commercially produced accounts book – you know, with 'Accounts' in red print on the cover. I nearly didn't open it, but it's as well that I did.

"It had been used for probably ten years to record the firearms – shotguns and pistols – that Mr Forbes-Kerr had bought. He was something of a collector – he'd purchased eleven pistols in that time, and none were shown as having been sold subsequently. The price paid for each, and the serial numbers, were recorded, but those were the only figures vaguely connected with 'accounts'.

"The book showed that in 1928, only a year or so before he died, the old boy bought a Liliput pistol. It was almost the last entry. He paid twenty-two pounds ten shillings for the pistol and two boxes of 6.35 mm ammunition. It came from a London dealer.

"Then the women took me to the gun room. No lock on the door. Several proper cabinets with a dozen or so shotguns – 12-bores and four-tens. Again, the cabinets were not locked.

"There was a sort of chest-of-drawers, and that's where his pistols were stored. I checked those present against the inventory. The only discrepancy is the Liliput – it isn't there. But there was one box of 6.35 mm ammunition, and none of the other pistols use that.

"I had the fingerprint outfit in the car, sir, so I dusted the drawers, and the gun room door, and the remaining box of ammo in case our man touched that.

"When I said I dusted for prints, I should say that the room itself was very dusty. The horizontal surfaces, like the top of the chest-of-drawers were covered, but they hadn't been disturbed in years. The maids told me that the room wasn't one they had to keep clean, and in fact neither had ever been inside it."

"I've brought the log book back with me sir.

"But the clincher is the serial number of the

Liliput, sir. It's recorded in the log book – and I telephoned Mr Brough to check the number on the pistol we found – it's the same."

"Well done indeed, Sergeant! Very thoughtful of you to look for dabs, too. It's only circumstantial against Owen, of course, but you've proved that the murder weapon came from Morlands. We'll check with Mrs F, but from what she told me, London guests haven't been entertained there since her husband died. That leaves the servants."

"Oh," added Gemmill, "I asked the maids if they had seen anyone near the gun room when the London staff were present a few weeks ago, but they said they hadn't."

"No, that would have been too much to hope for! But never mind – you found what I hoped you would.

"Right – we'll all go to Douglas House. I wonder – if we take Owen in for questioning, perhaps one of the other servants will remember him creeping up the stairs or doing something equally suspicious."

When the Yard officers rang the bell, it was Owen who came to open the door. As soon as the three were inside, and the front door closed again, Adair told the footman he was under arrest on suspicion of murder, and cautioned him. Gemmill put on handcuffs before the man had even taken in what the DCI had said.

"Take him to Vine Street, and book him in.

Don't talk to him, and don't answer if he speaks to you. But note anything he says, of course. If he asks for a solicitor, stall – I have a feeling that big guns will be arranged on his behalf, and I want him to have the best. I'll just talk to Mrs F and a few others here, and then I'll walk round and join you."

Only a couple of minutes had passed between entering the house and the door closing again behind the departing trio. Adair stood for a moment, wondering if there was any precedent for a visitor to wander unescorted along the hall and barge unannounced into the drawing room. Amused at the thought, he shrugged his shoulders and walked towards the drawing room. He could hear muffled voices through the door, as he tapped and went in.

Mrs Forbes-Kerr was sitting facing him, and near her were several of those he had interviewed recently. Those with their backs to the door, seeing the look of surprise on the face of their hostess, twisted around.

"Good morning, Chief Inspector. This is a surprise. I heard the front door bell, but who let you in?"

"Good morning, ladies and gentlemen. Samuel let me in, ma'am. I have something to report."

"Good, come and sit down, and tell us."

She indicated a very comfortable armchair, next to an identical one occupied by the Marchioness.

Adair glanced at each of the faces around him before speaking.

"I have just arrested Samuel Owen on suspicion of murder. He is being taken to Vine Street police station. In a little while I'll go and interview him. It is probable that I shall then charge him with the murder of Jocelyn Hardingham.

"I can't go into details at this stage, but suffice it to say that it can be shown that Owen certainly had a motive. I'd really rather that you refrain from too much speculation, but Lady Wymondham here already has some idea, and will be able to outline that."

Everybody except her husband stared at the Marchioness in surprise.

There was a silence in the room for a few seconds.

"Well," said Mrs Forbes-Kerr at last, "as Samuel is in my employ, I think it falls to me to arrange and finance his defence. Whatever he may have done, he is entitled to that."

"Very kind of you, ma'am," observed Adair. "I really shouldn't say this, but I have every sympathy with the man. However, one simply cannot go around taking the law into one's own hands – and especially not going as far as murder."

"No indeed," remarked Egerton. "Can't have anarchy. But if the man had good reason for what he did, then he should have the best counsel available. I know a couple of good solicitors,

Evelyn - would you like me to sort something out?"

"If you would, Travis, thank you."

"Perhaps it's as well Patrick has left the house, Evelyn," said the Marquis, as Egerton stood up and moved towards the door. "I'm not sure if barristers can nominate themselves for a brief, but I bet he'd have wanted to – even though presumably he couldn't have actually taken it, being almost involved."

Everyone smiled, and Adair thought he had learned something about the future judge.

Before I leave, ma'am, I'd like to speak to your servants – in a group, ideally. Also to Miss Barnes, if she is here. I won't take above five minutes of their time."

"Certainly, Chief Inspector. You're nearest the bell, Andrew; ring, if you please."

Lord Wymondham could reach the button without getting up, and pressed it hard.

That done, everyone sat looking at the DCI, although they each had a different thought.

Phoebe Wren spoke for the first time.

"I know you said you can't give details, Chief Inspector, but perhaps you can answer one question in case Elizabeth can't. You know what Jocelyn suggested to me. Had he done something really bad?"

"In a word, Miss Wren – yes."

Phoebe nodded slowly. Evelyn, who hand already apologised profusely for her maladroit efforts to match the pair, was about to do so again when the Butler appeared. He didn't have time to utter the traditional words, as Mrs Forbes-Kerr spoke first.

"Gather all the staff in the dining room, Morgan, and ask Miss Barnes to go there too. The Chief Inspector wishes to address you all."

"Very good, madam."

"Thank you, ma'am," said the DCI. "I'll very probably need formal statements from most of you sometime, but there is no hurry. I'll thank you all for your assistance, and say goodbye."

Adair caught up with the Butler in the hallway, and was directed to the dining room.

The silver here was even finer than that in Farncombe's house – and the artwork in considerably better taste.

Miss Barnes was the first to arrive, and he pointed her to a seat at the head of the table.

"I'm occasionally invited to eat in here, Chief Inspector, but I've never sat in this place before," she said with a little smile.

"Well, you won't have much time to savour it, Miss Barnes, and alas, there won't be any food."

The Cook and two maids arrived next, and again the DCI indicated that they should sit down. Within five minutes, all except Morgan were present. He returned a minute later.

"I can't find Samuel, sir; I think he must have slipped out of the house for something, although I have not approved such a move."

"Apologies, Mr Morgan, I should have

explained to you earlier what I'm going to tell you all now.

"A few minutes ago, I arrested Owen on suspicion of murder. He is now in Vine Street police station."

There were gasps from several of those present, and all looked shocked.

"Given that information, I now want you all to think very carefully about Tuesday evening, when your mistress held a dinner party. If any of you saw Samuel doing anything unusual; or if you saw him going upstairs at any time during the later part of the evening, you must say."

Adair looked at the faces around the table, but saw nothing to suggest anyone was going to volunteer information.

"I think we were all so busy the whole evening, sir," said Matthew, one of the other footmen, "it would have been impossible for any of us to notice what anyone else was doing."

"That is quite correct," intoned the Butler. "I was directing proceedings, so to speak, but I certainly could not testify as to who was doing what, and where they were, at any moment. Indeed, frankly, if Samuel disappeared for five or ten minutes, I should not have noticed."

"Very well. But there is something else. It may be that Samuel spoke to one or more of you about a lady friend of his – perhaps as much as eighteen months ago; perhaps much more recently. If so, please say."

Once again he scanned the faces as he spoke.

I judge from your faces that at least two of you have some knowledge. It may or may not have any bearing on the matter, but we need to hear about it anyway.

"One of my officers will come here again in the next day or so and speak to all of you – and in particular to you, Mrs Warren, and you, Miss O'Brien. Please do not hold anything back through some misplaced notion of loyalty.

"That is all, thank you."

CHAPTER 17

Adair walked the few hundred yards to Vine Street, and found Gemmill and Borthwick chatting to the Desk Sergeant in the foyer.

"Has he said anything?" enquired the DCI.

"Not a peep, sir," replied Gemmill, "seems quite happy, though."

"Okay. I just want a quick word with him – in his cell will do, if you can just open up for me please, Sergeant. One of you two come along."

Owen was sitting on the bunk, and stood up as the DCI came in. Space being limited, Gemmill, who had 'come along', remained in the doorway.

"Sit down again, Owen," instructed Adair. "I just came to say that I'm hoping you'll have a solicitor to advise you shortly. I want to give you the chance to talk to him before I interview you, so I'm going to wait for an hour or two."

"I can't afford a lawyer, sir."

"No, but your employer can, and she wants to do something for you."

"That's very good of her, sir. And good of you to wait."

"All right; we'll see who comes to represent you. I'll see you later."

The Custody Officer was still in the corridor, and the DCI indicated that he could lock the door again.

Back in the foyer, Adair looked at his watch.

"I anticipate that some high-powered solicitor will be here within half an hour, knowing the pull that Mrs F and her circle have. I doubt if he'll need more than another half hour to talk to his client, and probably less. It's not worth going back to the Yard. Let's go and get a cup of coffee in the mess room.

"If a mouthpiece arrives, Sergeant, please tell him that we're ready to interview his client as soon as he likes. And please inform your Super and the DDI that I've dumped another client in their cells!"

Over their coffee and cake, the DCI remarked that he couldn't really justify keeping both officers in Vine Street.

"But as it wouldn't be fair to send one of you back, you can both stay for the interview. Although I don't expect that to take very long."

"What do you think he'll say, sir?" queried Borthwick.

"Either he'll admit it straight away, which at this stage and with a lawyer present is unlikely. Or it'll be a 'no comment' interview. My money's on that."

"There's not much in the way of direct

evidence though, is there sir?" asked Gemmill.

"None, really. But plenty of circumstantial stuff. Enough for a jury – unless they take into account the motive and use that in their decision, which they really shouldn't."

The three talked about another concurrent case for the next twenty minutes, when a uniformed constable entered the room and came over to their table.

"Sarge says they're ready for you, sir."

Adair led his colleagues back and at the front desk the Custody Sergeant smiled.

"A Mr Fothergill arrived just after you went to the mess room, sir. He didn't need much time with the client. They're in interview room 3.

"Oh, and the Super says thanks!"

There was a constable on guard outside the interview room, and the DCI told him he could stand down, given the overwhelming number of policemen now present. The interview room was unusually large for its type, and there was ample room – and enough chairs – for five.

There were brief introductions, and everyone sat down, Fothergill – a very distinguished-looking man of about sixty – next to his client, and Adair flanked by his sergeants opposite.

Although Adair had not encountered the Solicitor before, he had heard the name – and his firm was very well known.

"I'd like to say at the outset that I appreciate

your holding off until I could get here, Chief Inspector," began Fothergill.

"Now, our position at present is that we'd like you to carry out your interview, in which no doubt you will be outlining the case against Mr Owen. You'll have questions for him, of course, and I reserve the right to advise him not to answer any particular one if I deem that to be in his interest."

"Understood, Mr Fothergill. Let me also say two things at the outset. First, should you require a break, with or without refreshments in the way of tea or coffee, just say. Second, your client was cautioned on arrest, and he has said absolutely nothing up to now. That caution is still in effect, Mr Owen, and my officers here will be noting down what I say, and what you say.

"Right. Tell us please how you became aware of the existence of the late Mr Hardingham."

"I think it was about January last year, sir. I was walking out with someone who worked in a house not far away. Her name was Aggie Yates. We saw each other about once a week – when our time off came together. I'd known her for maybe a year, and lately we'd been talking about finding somewhere we could work together, and then perhaps marry. Aggie wasn't happy in her place anyway, and I was thinking of asking Mrs Forbes-Kerr if Aggie could be considered for the next vacancy in Douglas House.

Then, one awful afternoon, Aggie told me

she had been raped by one of her master's guests, a few days before. She was crying when she told me, and kept going on about how she had wanted to keep herself for me. That's when she first mentioned the name Hardingham, sir."

"Don't call me 'sir'. I'm not your employer, nor your senior officer, nor your superior in any way. You are a citizen being interviewed by a policeman. Use Mr Adair, or Chief Inspector, or even nothing at all.

"So, did Aggie actually say that it was Hardingham who had assaulted her?"

"Yes. She said that several times. I wanted to go to the police, but she wouldn't have it. She said that Farncombe, her master, had given her fifty pounds to keep quiet. Around a year's wages. But also, she didn't want a lot of examinations and personal questions and so on – in fact that was why she had agreed to take the money and keep quiet."

"Understandable," said the DCI, "go on."

"Well, we carried on as we had been for another month or so, although she was still very upset. Then one afternoon we met in the park at our usual place, and I found her crying again. That was when she told me she was pregnant.

"Neither of us knew what to do. I'd have been happy to marry her, but where could we live? Anyway, she supposed the baby would have to go for adoption. She said she would speak to Farncombe, who might know how that could be arranged. She expected to lose her job soon anyway.

"That was the last time I saw her. She didn't turn up at our rendezvous the next week. I used the mistress's telephone to call her, and spoke to Sylvia – I'd met her a few times. She said she couldn't talk on the telephone, but agreed to meet me the next day. It was Sylvia who told me what had happened.

"I guessed that Hardingham and Farncombe had pushed my poor Aggie into having an abortion.

"I just didn't know what to do. I didn't have anyone to confide in really, although I did tell Cook and one of our maids what had happened. I didn't tell anyone the name, though. I had no proof – not even any proof that he was the father.

"I thought if I made unsub...unsubst..."

"Unsubstantiated accusations..." interjected Adair.

"Yes – that I'd not only lose my job but he could go after me for slander or something.

"I made some enquiries as best I could, and I heard only a few days later that Hardingham had left the country. That was over a year ago.

"Then a few weeks ago I discovered he was to be an overnight guest at Douglas House."

Owen stopped.

"You're doing very well, Mr Owen. Before you go any further, please tell us something else.

"Did Aggie tell you about the parties that were held in the Upper Brook Street house?"

"She did, but she never wanted to go into detail. She told me once that it must have been like those Roman orgies she'd read about. Sometimes there were upper-class ladies present, and other times the women were sort of prostitutes, I think. People always ended up in the bedrooms, whichever.

"Aggie said she and Sylvia were very well paid, and until the business with Hardingham she had never been, er, bothered. So she stayed. Held her nose, as it were.

"When Sylvia was telling me about Aggie's death, she also mentioned that the place was really like a brothel."

"Thank you. You might like to know that earlier today I charged Mr Farncombe with two offences. And a police officer has resigned after admitting accepting a bribe to turn a blind eye to things – including the circumstances of Aggie's death. He may also face criminal charges. Those matters came into my view while investigating Hardingham's murder, and although I carried out the arrest they aren't strictly my concern. However, I have suggested to my local colleagues that they may well be able to trace and prosecute the abortionist, if they do now what the disgraced police officer failed to do at the time."

"Thank you, Chief Inspector; that's good."

"So, do you want to tell us what you did when you realised you would soon be coming face-to-face with the man you hold responsible for

Aggie's rape and death?"

Fothergill intervened.

"Suppose you tell us first why other people were crossed off your list of suspects, Chief Inspector?"

"Certainly. At first, I assumed one of the other twelve guests killed Hardingham. Even the mistress of the house believed that must be so. As she said, Hardingham had never visited either Douglas House or Morlands, her country house, so none of the servants could have met him before.

"But then it turned out that none of the guests knew him either. Some knew him by name because they were acquainted with his father. A couple of others had met him while he was still at school – again via his father.

"None of these people had any reason to kill him. So, I belatedly turned to the staff.

"A rumour had reached us early on that Hardingham was amoral, and we learned about the abortion from Lord Hardingham. He didn't have any names, but a search of inquest records uncovered a few. We were lucky Aggie's was included, because the Coroner actually returned an open verdict. After that, basic police work gave us the name of Aggie's young man. And there it was."

Owen nodded sadly.

"That's given you something of a motive, for my client, Chief Inspector," said Fothergill, "and I assume in a big household like that the opportunity might arise.

"But what about means? Surely you're not suggesting that Mr Owen, with very little money and not many chances of getting out of the house for any length of time, knew where to find an illicit gun dealer and just went out and bought a pistol?"

Adair gave a faint smile.

"Oh no, Mr Fothergill. Nothing so difficult. Your client, along with most of the other Douglas House staff, went down to Morlands for a week at the beginning of this month. The late Mr Forbes-Kerr had a collection of pistols – all of which have lain untouched and unprotected since he died ten years ago.

"He owned a Liliput pistol of the appropriate calibre, bought along with two boxes of ammunition not long before his death. One box of the ammunition remains – the other box and the pistol have gone. And the serial number on the murder weapon – which we recovered from Douglas House – is the same as that on the one missing from Morlands.

"In the week that the London household were in Hampshire, only a small number of people could have appropriated the pistol. There were no guests. There was Mrs Forbes-Kerr herself – but she never left the drawing room during the time when the murder occurred. There was the Cook, and three maids. There were three footmen. Six of those seven people had never heard of Mr Hardingham before."

"But you, Mr Owen, had not only heard of him – you had a very good reason to hate him.

"I think a jury will have little doubt that you took the pistol, and that when Hardingham came into your purview a few days later, you took the opportunity to execute him.

"There were a couple of other things, which puzzled me until I realised it was you. The body was picked up from the floor and placed on the bed. And the towel which had been used to muffle the sound of the shot wasn't just left on the floor – it was neatly folded and hung over the back of a chair.

"With hindsight, those were the actions of a man who was used to making everything neat and orderly. Like a footman. Am I right?"

Owen sighed, and glanced sideways at his Solicitor. Fothergill gave a sort of shrug.

"You've heard the case – it's your decision now," he said.

"Yes, thank you," said Owen. "Well, you're quite right, Chief Inspector. Everything was exactly as you said. I wanted to admit this at once, but Mr Fothergill advised me to hear the evidence first. Then, as you heard, it was up to me. As I'd admitted my guilt to him, and refused to consider any suggestion of insanity, he said he wouldn't be able to act for me any further if I decided to plead not guilty and offer the defence of an alibi or anything. But he said he'd find other lawyers to help me if I chose to go down that path.

"But that would be ridiculous. I don't want to hang, so I'll have to hope the man who makes the final decision – the Home Secretary, is it? – feels that I don't have to join my Aggie just yet.

"I'd heard once about a verdict of justifiable homicide, but Mr Fothergill tells me that isn't available in my case. Anyway, I have no regrets about what I've done."

There was a silence in the room.

Eventually Adair spoke.

"There will be an inquest into Hardingham's death next week. The verdict can hardly be anything but one of murder, and I am sure that the jury will name you as the responsible person. I can just about visualise a bloody-minded but sympathetic jury bringing in a verdict of justifiable homicide, but that certainly won't be one of the options offered by the Coroner. Even if they did bring in such a verdict, it would actually have no effect on how your case will proceed.

"My personal view is that you are wise not to try going down the insanity route. As Mr Fothergill may have explained, the 'Rules' used in criminal trials state that a defendant is assumed sane unless it is proved otherwise. And you – or your barrister – would have to show that either you didn't know what you were doing, or that you didn't know it was wrong. There are a dozen ways in which the Crown could show that either of those hypotheses is absurd.

"My personal opinion doesn't count, but I do

have considerable sympathy for you. However, we simply can't tolerate personal vendettas, and that is why I have to charge you now.

"Samuel Owen, I charge you with the murder of Jocelyn Hardingham, at Douglas House, Piccadilly, between the 29th and 30th of August this year, contrary to the Common Law.

"You'll appear before the Vine Street magistrate in the morning. Good luck to you, Mr Owen.

"Do you want more time with your client, Mr Fothergill?"

"A few more minutes, if you please."

"Very well; carry on in here. I'll arrange for an officer to remain outside. I'll no doubt see you in court tomorrow. Good afternoon."

***

In the foyer, the DCI instructed the Sergeant to put the constable back on the interview room door, and said to his colleagues, "Let's get back to the Yard."

"Never seen you so nice to a defendant, sir," said Borthwick. "I reckon you were more sympathetic than you would be if you were interviewing someone with a faulty rear light on his car," he added daringly – immediately realising he had overstepped the mark.

Gemmill, at the wheel, waited to hear his friend receive a sharp rebuke.

Neither man had need to worry, as the DCI

laughed.

"Quite right. I think Owen has been dealt a particularly bad hand in life. Of course, he went far too far."

"Will he hang sir?" asked Borthwick. "Like you, I'm very sympathetic."

"Me too," added Gemmill.

"Well, let's assume that at trial he maintains his intention to plead guilty. That is a vanishingly rare situation in a capital matter, of course. As you may know, in those particular circumstances the prosecution still has to produce evidence, in effect to support that plea, and technically the jury still has to convict him.

"In the witness box I shall do my best to show that Owen had very good reason to loathe his victim. That won't help him escape the mandatory death penalty, of course, but the jury might add a recommendation for mercy.

The Home Secretary may or may not take note of that. He will certainly consult the trial judge. And whether I'm asked to or not, I shall be submitting a report. If there was ever a case where clemency is merited, it must be this one.

****

BOOKS BY THIS AUTHOR

The Bedroom Window Murder

Book 1 in the Philip Bryce series, set in 1949.

The Courthouse Murder

Book 2 in the Philip Bryce series.

The Felixstowe Murder

Book 3 in the Philip Bryce series.

Multiples Of Murder

Book 4 in the Philip Bryce series.

Death At Mistram Manor

Book 5 in the Philip Bryce series.

Machinations Of A Murderer

Book 6 in the Philip Bryce series.

Suspicions Of A Parlourmaid And The Norfolk Railway Murders

Book 7 in the Philip Bryce series.

This Village Is Cursed

Book 8 in the Philip Bryce series.

The Amateur Detective

Book 9 in the Philip Bryce series.

Demands With Menaces

Book 10 in the Philip Bryce series.

Murder In Academe

Book 11 in the Philip Bryce series.

Murder In The Rabid Dog

Book 12 in the Philip Bryce series.

The King's Bench Walk Murder And Death In The Boardroom

Book 13 in the Philip Bryce series.

Death Of A Safebreaker

Not in a series. A murder mystery, set in 1937.

Death Of A Juror

Not in a series. A murder mystery, set in 1936.

The Missing Schoolgirls

Book 1 in the David Adair series, set in 1938.

The Numbered Murders

Book 2 in the David Adair series.

The Failed Lawyer

A short period in the life of a young man.

The Devon Murders

Book 14 in the Philip Bryce series.

Printed in Dunstable, United Kingdom